The Number You Have Reached

The Number You Have Reached

Melvin Sterne

LAMAR UNIVERSITY press

ISBN: 978-0-9850838-4-7
Library of Congress Control Number: 2013954489
Manufactured in the United States of America
Cover Design: Lisa Craig

Lamar University Press
Beaumont, Texas

Dedication

There are half-a-hundred people to whom I am wildly indebted for these stories and this publication including, especially, Jerry Craven, Editor of Lamar University Press, and the editors of the various journals who published my individual stories. There are, too, those friends and teachers who helped me along the way including Bob Butler, Pam Houston, Dick Dunn, Julianna Baggott, David Bosworth, Steve Quig, and Marilyn Smith, among others. But there is one person, for good or bad, without whom this book would never have been written.

To Miss Iris Cornflower, wherever you may be.

Books from Lamar University Press

Jean Andrews, *High Tides, Low Tides: the Story of Leroy Colombo*
Alan Berecka, *With Our Baggage*
David Bowles, *Flower, Song, Dance: Aztec and Mayan Poetry*
Robert Murray Davis, *Levels of Incompetence: An Academic Life*
Jeffrey Delotto, *Voices Writ in Sand*
Mimi Ferebee, *Wildfires and Atmospheric Memories*
Ken Hada, *Margaritas and Redfish*
Michelle Hartman, *Disenchanted and Disgruntled*
Lynn Hoggard, *Motherland: Stories and Poems from Louisiana*
Dominique Inge, *A Garden on the Brazos*
Gretchen Johnson, *The Joy of Deception*
Tom Mack and Andrew Geyer, editors, *A Shared Voice*
Dave Oliphant, *The Pilgrimage, Selected Poems: 1962-2012*
Janet McCann, *The Crone at the Casino*
Erin Murphy, *Ancilla*
Harold Raley, *Louisiana Rogue*
Carol Coffee Reposa, *Underground Musicians*
Jim Sanderson, *Trashy Behavior*
Jan Seale, *Appearances*
Jan Seale, *The Parkinson Poems*

For more information on these and other books, go to
www.LamarUniversityPress.Org

Also by Melvin Sterne:
Zara, a novel set in India

Acknowledgments

I am grateful to the editors of the following journals for publishing stories that appear in this collection:

"Thanksgiving," *South Carolina Review*
"The End of the World," *Natural Bridge*
"Bread," *Kaleidoscope*
"Split Decision," *Crucible*
"Dead Water," *Blue Mesa Review*
"The Heart-Smart Diet," *Willow Springs*
"The Funeral," *Mochilla Review*
"Warriors," *Watchword*
"The Couch," *Amarillo Bay*
"The Number You Have Reached," *StorySouth*

CONTENTS

Thanksgiving

First April stopped loving me. Then she ran off with the guy who read the gas meter. I heard they got married in Reno. They drove down in the gas company truck, so it was all over the county paper, and folks around here talked it up for weeks. And if that wasn't enough, all this happened right before Thanksgiving. I had turkey with her mom, anyway. "She'll come back," Helen said, patting me on the arm.

A few years later I heard April left the gas meter guy and ran off with her yoga instructor. After that, I lost track. Ten years went by and I almost gave up on her. Then one day she called and said she was passing through and wondered could she stop over.

Checkerboard is not the kind of place people pass through by accident. It's not on the road to anywhere, but I didn't question her on that. I said okay and a few hours later, there she was, bouncing up the front steps with a big grin on her face, like she'd just got home from shopping. Except for the little boy tagging along behind her, she looked just like she did the day she left me. I didn't know she had a kid. He was a pale little six-year-old, a redhead, at the gangly stage—all arms and legs, knees and elbows. He wore blue jeans rolled up over his shoes, a red tee shirt, black high-top sneakers, and a blue cap with a silver star on it.

"The place looks the same, Frank," April said, and it did. "Looks like you haven't changed a thing," she said, and I hadn't. We sat on the same couch and looked out the same window with the same curtains pulled back with the same rope sashes she'd made because we were too cheap to buy the ones that came with the curtains we bought at J.C. Penney's.

"You look funny," Tommy said, dangling his feet from the couch. "What happened to your head?"

April leaned over, slapped Tommy on the thigh, and hissed in his ear, "It's not nice to talk about other people, Tommy. Everybody looks different somehow."

"It's all right," I said. "It's true. You see, Tommy, my grandpa was a Flathead Indian, and my grandma was a grizzly bear. They lived in a cave up on Mount Baldy. That made my dad half-and-half, and me a quarter. I got the bear's head from my grandma's side of the family. But if you think I'm ugly, you should see my sister."

"What's wrong with her?" Tommy asked.

"She's covered with hair and got claws this long." I gestured with my hands, making my fingers out to be claws. "She lives up on the mountain and only comes down when she gets hungry."

April rolled her eyes and looked away. She knows how I am when I get started with my stories.

"What does she eat?" Tommy asked, inching closer to his mom.

"Mostly Popsicles. But she'll eat anything if she's hungry enough. See that stump out in the yard?"

Tommy looked out the window.

"That used to be a big pine tree. She came by last week when I wasn't home and ate the whole thing."

"Did not."

"Yup," I said, "Pine cones and all. You can still see the teeth-marks if you look at the stump."

"Looks like chain saw cuts to me," April said. "Next thing you're going to tell me is what she didn't eat she stacked around the side of the house to dry."

"Nope, she ate the whole thing. The only thing sis won't eat is my cooking."

Tommy perked up and then asked, "What's wrong with your cooking?"

"My cooking is so bad, I throw it out and the coyotes won't eat it."

"Can I have a Popsicle? Mom said you always had Popsicles."

"Sure," I said. "I got a whole freezer full." I got Popsicles and we sat on the couch and ate them.

"Still work at the mill?" April asked.

"Yup. You know me. Steady Eddy. Eight-for-eight, never late."

"Have you made foreman yet?"

I laughed. "No. Dean-o still runs the show. He'll be there 'til he retires, or dies. But he treats me okay. It's still the best job in town."

"More like the only job in town."

"How 'bout you," I said, leaning forward on my elbows. "How you keeping these days?"

April stroked her hair back from her eyes and took a deep breath.

She's in her middle thirties, but she's got the kind of young looks that still get her ID'd in bars. She's petite, with dark, smooth skin. She cuts her hair short in a pageboy look, and it never looks out of style on her. Other than a few fine lines around her eyes, she looked just like the morning I saw her last. It was a Friday. She cooked bacon and eggs for breakfast and packed my lunch. I kissed her on my way out and she reminded me that we had a date for dinner with her mom that night. When I came home she was gone—no note—no nothing. I called the cops and filled out a missing person report, climbed the walls all weekend. It wasn't until the gas company reported their truck stolen that we put two and two together. I got a card in the mail a few weeks later from San Antonio. Sorry, it said. Since we weren't officially married, there was no divorce. She was gone, and that was that.

"I'm fine, Frank," she said, and then she laughed and leaned back into the couch and covered her eyes. "I'm okay. Well, actually, things aren't so good, but I'll get by. Hell," she said, and then she looked at Tommy and said, "Whoops."

Tommy said, "Five cents, please," and held out his hand.

April opened her purse and felt around in it. Then she got off the couch and sat cross-legged on the floor and emptied it out in front of her and rooted through the contents. There were car keys and a tube of lipstick, a comb, some Kleenex, a foil pack with a condom, a stick of chewing gum, a little blue plastic vial of breath freshener, a tiny stuffed bear attached to a key ring with no keys on it, a coin that looked like a St. Christopher, and a postage-stamp-sized photo of a dark-complected man with a short beard and sad, brown eyes. At the bottom of the pile were some coins and April sorted through them until she found a dime. "He fines me every time I swear," she said, handing it to Tommy. "This is for next time, too, honey, okay?" Tommy nodded and slipped the dime into his pocket. April looked up at me and said, "Actually, my life's a wreck. I was wondering if I could stay a few days while I sort things out."

"Sure," I said.

April arrived in a green VW pop-top camper with Tennessee tags, a crumpled fender, and one headlight dangling from a wire like a cartoon eye popped out of its socket. I helped her carry her bags into the guest room. "Makes it kind of hard to drive at night," I said, standing in the driveway and kicking at the tires. They were so bald the fabric showed through.

April laughed nervously. "Yes it does."

"Do you need to park it around back?" I said. "Maybe in the garage?"

"No. It's not stolen, if that's what you mean. I mean, I have permission to take it. Sort of. Anyway, I don't think it's been reported stolen, and even if it was, he wouldn't press charges. We'd just call it a misunderstanding."

"A misunderstanding?"

"Look, I don't feel like talking about it right now. If it makes you feel better, you can park it in the garage, if you want."

I parked the van in the garage and called a friend in the junk business and he said to hammer out the ding he would round up a used headlight assembly for me on the cheap. I asked April if she was hungry and Tommy looked up at her but said nothing. April said she was, so I drove them to the Royal Fork in Bozeman and sprung for an all-you-can-eat buffet. Tommy ate like he had a hollow leg and I kidded him about it, pulled his hat down over his eyes and rubbed him on the tummy. "Where are you putting all that?" I asked. He squealed and wriggled away.

April asked me to stop at a 7-11 on the edge of town, and she bought a bottle of wine and drank the whole thing on the way back. When we got home she said she was tired and wanted to sleep, so I made up the bed in the spare bedroom and she and Tommy laid down. I went out in the garage and hammered on the VW for a while, and when I came back in, Tommy was watching TV.

"Hello, sport," I said, "would you like another Popsicle?" He nodded. I got one for me, too, and sat down on the couch beside him. "You watch much TV?"

He shook his head. "We sleep in the van, mostly. So we don't got one."

"Do you like camping? I bet you got to see some beautiful places."

He shrugged his shoulders. "I'm not supposed to talk about it," he said.

"Talk about what?"

"Where we been."

"I didn't ask where you were, I just asked if you saw some pretty places."

"I guess so."

"What's your favorite?"

"Cal'fornia, but I'm not supposed to tell you that."

"Why?"

"Mom says it's a secret."

"Then I won't tell. What did you like the most about it?"

"It was sunny a lot, and warm. When it's cold or rainy I can't go out."

"What do you like to do?"

Tommy squirmed on the couch. "I like to play soccer. I used to play on a team."

"What else do you like?"

"When it's rainy I like to read."

"You read all ready? Who taught you to read?"

"I don't know. I think I always knew."

* * *

Tommy went to bed and I poured myself a beer and went out on the back porch. The wind blew steady down from the north and there was a chill in the air. A few dry leaves blew by. The porch swing swayed in the breeze, its chain creaking softly.

I went to bed and was almost asleep when I heard a clunk on the front porch. It's nothing, I thought, it's April getting a drink of water, or Tommy can't sleep. But after a while I knew I wouldn't sleep until I checked it out, so I went to the front door and looked outside. There was a man standing on the porch. I opened the door. "What do you want?" I asked.

The man seemed surprised to see me. He was about my height, but skinny, with a short, scruffy beard. He wore Levis and a blue denim shirt, cowboy boots, a cowboy hat pulled down low over his eyes. "Is April there?" he asked.

"April who?"

"You know who I mean."

"There's nobody here that concerns you," I said. "Go on back where you came from."

I shut the door but he stuck his boot in the jam.

"What are you...drunk?" I asked.

He pushed the hat up from his eyes. "She can't run forever," he said.

I flipped on the porch light and saw him more clearly then. He was not the same man as the photograph in April's purse.

"Has she told you about the canoe?" he asked.

"No."

He stepped towards me like he was going to come in but I caught him under the throat with my left hand and shoved him down the steps. He sprawled on his back in the yard. "I'm gonna get my shotgun," I said. "Best be gone when I get back."

I closed the door and paused in the hallway. I could hear him through the door, laughing, big belly laughs coming from the front yard. I didn't know why I said I was going to get a gun. The beer must have gone to my head. I have a shotgun but I don't keep it loaded. I wasn't even sure I had shells. I sat down in the living room and later, when I looked outside, he was gone. He's crazy, I thought, now that's just perfect.

The door to the back bedroom opened and April peeked out. "What was that?" she asked.

"Nothing," I said. "A fella got lost and needed directions."

* * *

The next morning was Saturday and I baked biscuits, cooked up bacon and eggs and hash browns. Tommy was hungry, but not so hungry as the night before. April didn't eat much at all, she sat in the swing on the back porch sipping her coffee and looking at the mountains. To the north they're covered with pine and fir, and they're a pleasant, hazy blue. Right outside town the hills were clear-cut years ago and eroded to bare, brown rock. But the Musselshell River flows down from the north, through a gap in the hills, and the valley there is wide, green and pretty, and we used to go up in the summer and pick blackberries, or fish the beaver dams for brookies.

"You think the blackberries are still out?" April asked.

I sipped my coffee and thought about it a while.

She knew darn good and well the blackberries were out—she grew up here, too—and I took the question to be a sly reminder of all the fun we used to have. Picking blackberries meant picnic lunch in the meadows, a roll in the hay, and then, late in the day, we might pick a few berries. We fished the same way. Back when April and I were dating, and her mother was still alive, I remember Helen asking us what kind of fish we intended to catch, seeing as how we sometimes forgot our gear.

6

"A few," I said, searching her face for a sign.

We went picking that afternoon and came home with our fingers and tongues stained purple, our arms and legs scratched and full of stickers. That night I made fresh blackberry ice cream and Tommy, who had never made ice cream before, sat up on the counter with me and helped, amazed. It was like he'd seen god. So this is where ice cream comes from. When we were done, he thought I was the greatest. He was worn out from hiking and fell asleep on the couch watching football. April tucked him into bed and then came out and sat with me. I lit a fire and poured us a couple of glasses of wine. After a while April said, "I never wrote you about him, did I?" and I said, "No."

"He was from my second marriage. That was the one to Vaarni, the yoga instructor, you knew about him, right?"

I nodded. Checkerboard is a small town and I saw April's mom at least once a week, if not for dinner, then because she ran the only gas station in town. She kept me pretty well up on things and always ended our visits with a motherly pat on the arm and her assurance that, "April will be back, someday, you know. She just needs time to sort things out." She was always good to me—Helen was. I suppose I was like a son to her. She had a son, once—older than April—but he died in a helicopter crash in Desert Storm. So when she took sick, I looked after her until she died. And even though she left the station to me, I sold it and wired the money to April. It didn't feel right keeping it. I was doing okay, and I was pretty sure April needed the money more than me.

"The problem was that Vaarni had had a vasectomy."

"That does complicate things."

"So I got divorced, again, and married Flip six months later in Denver. He's not Tommy's dad, either. Of course, Tommy doesn't know any of this."

"Of course," I said. "And how did you meet Flip?"

"He was an exotic dancer. I'm sorry, I shouldn't trouble you with all this. You don't want to know."

April changed into a man's tee shirt that she wore for a nightgown. The tee shirt had a picture of a candy-apple-red eighteen wheeler on the front of it with the words: *Big Red Rolls for You!* written underneath. The shirt hung down to her knees but her nipples showed through where it rubbed against her breasts.

She took her wine out on the porch and turned her back to me, leaned against the railing and looked at the moon. The tee shirt rode up on her thighs and I thought her legs were still fine. She always had good legs. Her breath came out in a faint cloud that hung over her and reminded me of a halo. It was an odd image and for some reason I remembered that Mary Magdalene was a reformed prostitute.

April stood up on her tiptoes and arched her back like a cat, the tee shirt climbing up almost to her ass. Her skin was perfect, her thighs tight and tan, without a trace of cellulite. I popped a woody and had to wriggle on the couch so it didn't stick out. She looked over her shoulder and saw that I was looking at her, and then she turned away and stood on her right leg and lifted her left foot and scratched the back of her right calf.

I couldn't take it any more—I tossed my wine and pecked April on the cheek good night. I crawled into bed and tugged the covers up tight around me, but before I fell asleep the door creaked and April appeared, silhouetted in the doorway. She slipped the tee shirt over her head and climbed into bed with me. "You don't have to do this," I said. She stopped my talking with a warm, wet kiss. After we made love we cuddled on the bed and I whispered, "Stay with me," but she was already asleep.

* * *

In the middle of the night I heard the garage door open and I reached for April but she was gone. I slipped on a pair of shorts and looked down the hall. The nightlight was on in the guest bedroom. I crept to the door and peeked inside, saw April curled up under the covers with Tommy. I went to the hall closet and took down the shotgun and a flashlight. I found three shells in a shoebox and stuffed them in the magazine. I slipped out the back door and snuck around the side of the house. There was an old 4x4 pickup truck in the drive, and a man sitting in the garage wrapping a chain around the axle of April's VW.

I chambered a shell and said, in my deepest TV voice, "Stay very still." The man froze. I looked around the yard carefully to make sure he was alone, and when I was satisfied I walked around and shined the light in his face. It was the same fella who was on my porch the night before. "You're about half-stupid aren't you?" I said.

"Can I get up now?" he asked.

"No," I said, and I used my foot to push him face down on the concrete. "Keep your hands where I can see 'em." He did and I laid the barrel of the shotgun on the back of his head and said, "Very still," and he nodded.

I patted him down and he said, "I'm not packing."

I said, "That's nice, but I'm going to make sure just the same." I pulled his boots off, too, because sometimes folks hide a pistol or a knife in 'em. But he was clean, and when I was sure I said, "Okay, you can get up."

He sat up and pulled his boots on. "Mind if I smoke?"

"Go ahead."

He took a pack out of his shirt pocket and dug a lighter out of his jeans. He flicked the lighter and his face lit up in the flame. "I've got some beer in my truck. Would you like one? They're cold."

"Sure," I said. "What the hell," and we walked over to the truck, me on one side and him on the other. He had a cooler on the seat and he opened it and handed me a bottle of Coors. The cab was littered with bottles. I leaned the shotgun against the door and we sat down and he turned on the radio. The only station he could find was a country station out of Bozeman and it sounded tinny. After a while I said, "You want to tell me about it?"

"You've been with her," he said. "I can smell it on you."

"Look. I've known April since we were kids, and she used to be my old lady. What we do in my house is our business, and since I got a shotgun and you don't, I get to ask the questions. So tell me, what the hell are you doing here?"

He didn't say anything, and I started getting fidgety. "Okay. We'll play twenty questions. Are you from Tennessee?"

"Enid, Oklahoma."

"Well that explains a lot. Is your name Flip?"

He raised the eyebrow over his right eye and looked at me. "Flip's dead."

"Oh," I said. "I suppose I'm sorry to hear that. Besides stalking April, what brings you to Montana?"

"Tommy's my son. I love April, but I want Tommy back."

"Your son?"

"Yeah."

"So what are you gonna do, kidnap the car and trade it for the kid?"

"No."

"What, then?"

"Did you ever break a horse?"

"No. I'm not much into horses."

"Well you can't just throw a saddle on them and ride, and you can't tie them down, either. You got to hobble them, tie their legs so they'll stand in one place. Then you can get close enough to rub a blanket on them, get them used to the smell. After a while you slip a bridle on, get 'em used to being touched. When they get over being afraid, you saddle break 'em."

"Have you tried going to court?"

"Sure, but every time I find out where she is, she runs off again."

"So you figure you steal the van, she's got to stay put?"

"Exactly."

"Listen. I got no control over April—never have. But if I promise to try to make her sit still for a while, will you promise not to come sneaking around anymore?"

"That would be mighty decent of you," he said, offering me his hand. "My name's Jake."

"Frank," I said. I shook his hand. "Where're you staying?"

"Motel Six in Billings."

"Go home. Get some sleep."

I finished my beer and dropped the empty onto the floor, climbed out of the truck and slung the shotgun over my shoulder.

"One more thing," Jake said.

"What's that?"

"Did she tell you about the canoe?"

"No. What's up with the canoe?"

"She didn't tell you?"

"No."

"It's a lie. She killed that fella. Don't believe a word she says."

"You're drunk, Jake," I said. "Go home." As he drove away I whispered, "And stay there."

* * *

Sunday morning I slept late. April and Tommy woke me with breakfast in bed. April shuttled back and forth from the kitchen bringing pancakes and syrup and bacon and refilling my coffee. Tommy bounced up and down on the bed until he upset the tray and spilled our orange juice. Then he started to cry. April made it worse by snapping at him. Tommy really started bawling, then, and he headed for his room. I spilled my coffee to make him feel better, dumped it right over, and he stopped at the door. That really set April off. "You are two of a kind," she said.

"No big deal," I said. "Honest. Sheets were due for a wash anyway." I looked at Tommy and winked. "I wash my sheets once a year whether they need it or not."

"Ewww," April said, wrinkling her nose.

"Ewww," Tommy said, giggling.

April gathered the sheets and hauled them to the laundry room. Do you mind if I throw a few things in with these?" she asked.

"Make yourself at home."

Later that afternoon we drove to the junkyard and picked up the headlight assembly for the van. My buddy, Ernie, runs the place, he's a big Swede who used to work at the mill and started scrapping cars on the side. He started out with a tow truck working weekends, but it got so profitable that he quit the mill and went into the junk business full time. He picks up wrecks and impounds off the interstate, DWI's, the occasional recovered stolen car. He charges storage by the day and often, by the time folks get around to picking their cars up, the fees are more than the car is worth, so he gets them for nothing. He fixes up the ones he can and sells them. The rest he lays out in neat rows in what used to be the laydown yard of a sawmill that went belly-up. He had a half dozen VW vans. "The dead heads used to leave 'em regular as clockwork," he said. "They were dependable as geese. Every summer I'd bag one or two. But now that Jerry's gone, they're getting harder to come by."

I took that to mean he was going to jack the price on me, but then April came around the corner and Ernie's face lit up. "Well, lookee who's back! The prodigal daughter has returned. Good to see you, girl." And then turning to me he asked, "So does this mean you two are an item again?"

I opened my mouth but April cut me off laughing. "We're old friends," she said. "I'm just passing through."

"Well I'll give you the old friends price then," Ernie said, which was next-to-nothing. "Provided you come for dinner sometime this week."

I looked at April and she shrugged her shoulders.

We used to do a lot of this stuff after we got out of high school. I couldn't tell you how many weekends we spent listening to Lynryd

Skynyrd and ZZ Top, passing a bong and a bottle of Wild Turkey around up in Ernie and Eleanor's cabin out Sulfur Springs Road. Ernie and Eleanor are still together. They've got four kids now, and I know Eleanor doesn't do the wild thing anymore. I think Ernie still sells a little grass on the side, though I haven't smoked a joint in years, so I couldn't say for sure. The cabin burned down a while back, and Ernie built a house on the hill overlooking the junkyard.

"Sure," April said. "That would be great."

"You still make enchiladas?" Ernie asked. "You used to make the best enchiladas."

"Of course I do. I'll make us a double batch."

About that time Tommy came around the corner with a black puppy in his arms, the mother and the rest of the puppies following him. Before April could shout, "Put that thing down!" Tommy was toe to toe with her shouting, "Can I keep him? Can I? Can I? He's the best one and he followed me so I have to take him. You never let me have a dog."

Ernie busted out laughing.

The mama dog ran circles around Tommy. She was a scrawny, high-strung lab-cross with a prickly ridge of hair running down her spine like a razorback, a little white patch on her throat. The pups were still in the fuzzball stage and it was hard to tell what they might grow up to look like. The rest of the brood sat down in the dirt beside their mama, wobbling around and biting one another's tails. But the pup in Tommy's arms rested like he'd been born there.

"The daddy's a shepherd from across the road," Ernie said. "So they got some good blood in 'em."

"I don't care if he was the first dog to walk on the moon," April replied, "We ain't getting a dog."

April took the pup from Tommy and held him by the nape of his neck. He looked at her while the mama yelped and nipped at April's free hand. Tommy sat down in the dirt and started to bawl. I took the pup from April and looked at his feet, felt around his rib cage, and squeezed his jaw to make him show me his teeth.

"Tommy's got a good eye for a dog," I said. "He's the pick of the litter. Got more lab in him than shepherd. Gonna be a big one."

"Her daddy was a Newfie," Ernie said. "She was the runt of the litter, which was why I got stuck with her. You know, you'd be doing me a big favor taking him off my hands. I had to drown the last batch."

That started Tommy off bawling again, and he snatched the pup and held it protectively to his chest with one hand while he fought off the mother with the other. "We can't let him drown Newton," he said. "You got to let me keep him."

"You're a cruel man," I said.

"He's probably got fleas," April said. "Or worms." April sat down on her haunches and took the pup from Tommy and set him down at arm's length. "Honey, she said, "we got no place for a dog."

The pup wobbled back to Tommy and Tommy took him in his arms and turned to me. "Mr. Frank," he said, "you got a place for a dog. Please?"

* * *

Newton peed on my carpet first thing after he got in the house. I rolled up a newspaper and whacked him over the head with it, rubbed his nose in the wet spot, and tossed him out in the backyard. That set Tommy to howling again, until I explained that I loved Newton, too, but we couldn't have him peeing all over the house. And the newspaper didn't really hurt, it just scared him up a bit, and to illustrate the point I whacked Tommy a few times and then got down on all fours and let him whack me. He whacked me pretty good, whereupon I reminded him I was part bear and chased him around the house growling until I caught him and tickled him half to death. I told Tommy it was his job to clean up after Newton and I showed him how.

After that Tommy and Newton were inseparable. They spent most of their time outside and when they came in, Tommy was always careful to watch for signs that Newton needed out. They ate supper together on the back porch. We warned Tommy that Newton was still too young to eat grownup food and he seemed to understand, but I think he cheated when we weren't looking. They played until dark and then they came in and curled up in front of the fireplace and fell asleep. I carried Tommy off to bed and April laid Newton down on a towel on the floor, but when we went in to check on them, they were both on the bed and we were all right with that.

April went off to the garage to fetch a bottle of wine she had stashed in the VW and after a while I went out after her and found her smoking a joint around the side of the house. "I hope you don't mind," she said, and

I said that I didn't, even though I kind of did.

April held the joint out to me, but I shook my head. "It's been years. No sense starting back now."

"They drug test at the mill?"

"Yeah, but only for cause. I'd probably get off if they caught me. Half the crew is stoned to the gills."

"Why'd you quit?"

"Got tired of feeling stupid."

"Isn't that the point?"

"To feel stupid?"

"To stop thinking about things."

"I suppose, if your thoughts make you uncomfortable."

"Mine do."

"There's other ways, you know."

"Like what?"

"I don't know, but there must be."

"I ain't going to no counselor." April sucked on the joint and held it in. After a minute she exhaled a cloud of blue smoke and it clung to her with that halo effect again. "A miracle might help."

The days were getting shorter, the nights cold. While we watched, the frost made spidery silver lines on the dry leaves and on the edges of the windows. Goosebumps raised on April's arms. I thought about offering her a sweater, but I didn't want my clothes smelling like dope.

"What are you looking at?" April asked.

"You," I said. "You got a halo."

April looked up and then turned around and looked behind her. "I smoke dope and you see things. Only angels get halos, and I sure as hell ain't no angel."

"Do you remember when we were together?"

"Don't go getting sentimental on me."

"But do you remember?"

"Course I do."

"Was I good to you?"

"Sure, Frank, you're a swell guy. I thought about you lots. You'd make a great husband, a great father. A girl would be lucky to have a guy like you. You oughta get married someday."

"Then why'd you leave?"

"I don't know," she said, and then she laughed. "I've only got one

14

weakness…it's temptation I can't resist!"

"But it wasn't me? It wasn't anything I did?"

"No, Frank, it wasn't you. I was stupid, and young. I got bored. I started fooling around with Wally while you were at work, and then I felt guilty about it. I knew I couldn't give you what you deserve. It wasn't that I didn't want to—it just ain't in me."

"Can I be the judge of that?" I asked.

"No, not when it comes to me you can't. Can we go inside? I'm cold."

We went inside and then April remembered that she went out to get a bottle of wine in the first place, so she went back and got that, and then we sat down on the couch. I got up and built a fire while she fooled around with the corkscrew. "I bought a couple of bottles of this on sale in Omaha," she said. "It was supposed to be really good, but I didn't realize I needed a corkscrew to open them. I been meaning to buy one ever since, but I keep forgetting. It's easier just to buy another jug. I spent a few days outside of Laramie and got so thirsty that one night I took a rock and busted the top off a bottle and drank it down." She giggled. She was slurring her speech.

I almost had the fire going when I heard the cork pop and April shouted: "Shit!" She spilled the wine down the front of her shirt and got some on the couch, but it wasn't too bad. I blotted it up and stood back and looked at it. "Don't worry about it," I said. "It's an old couch."

April wadded up her shirt and threw it on the floor. "I didn't like that shirt much, anyhow. It was a present from a guy I didn't like."

I sat down, careful to keep the wet spot between us, and then April got up. She was wearing old jeans and a black, spaghetti-string, clamshell bra, the kind that pushes a girl's tits up and makes the most of them. She picked up the shirt and threw it in the fire. Then she said "Fuck!" and grabbed a fire poker and took it out, burned her foot stamping on it.

I laughed.

After she put the fire out she reached in the shirt pocket and pulled out a baggy of bud. "Thank God" she said. She threw the shirt back in the fire. "Do you mind if I roll another one?"

"Do you do that stuff in front of Tommy?"

"No. Well, sometimes, but he doesn't know what it is."

"Go ahead."

April rolled another joint and when she was done I asked, "So what's the story about the canoe?"

She had just lit the joint and she coughed hard, almost fell off the couch. "He's been here, huh?" she said.

"Who?"

"You know who I mean."

"How could I possibly know who you mean?"

"Well, he's full of shit," she said, "and besides that, he's crazy. He says I killed Flip, but he's just trying to blackmail me into marrying him. I shouldn't have slept with him. I don't know what I was thinking. I must have been drunk. Anyway, if he comes around again, let me know. I'll get another restraining order."

"So did you?"

"What?"

"Kill Flip?"

"Hell no! Flip killed himself. He quit taking his medication. He tried it before. This time there was nobody around to stop him." April took a deep breath and sighed. "I met Flip in Atlanta. I was working as a stripper at Peaches. Don't look at me like that, where else can a girl with no diploma make 200 bucks a night? Flip worked there too, but only on ladies' night. He was a hunk, but lost. He was like a big, dumb puppy. Except when he danced. Boy could he dance. He could do things... Well, anyway, he was good. And he was a sweet guy, too, but clueless. He had been abused by his father and his uncle, so he was confused about his sexuality and stuff. He had issues. We started hanging out. I liked him. He was gentle. He wasn't all over me like most guys are. He liked to go rafting on those slow, muddy southern rivers. Did I tell you he was an ex-junkie? That was why he didn't like taking his medicine. He didn't believe in changing the way you feel with chemicals. He wanted to do it himself, naturally.

"Anyway, Flip and I decided to make a clean break from stripping and drugs and all. This was about a year ago, in the spring. In the meantime, I had met this Okie at Peaches and he had a crush on me. He's got an inheritance—oil money or something—and he doesn't have to work, so he just drives around the country hanging out. He wanted to marry me, too. I don't know what it is with men. You sleep with them once and they think they own you. Okay, I shouldn't have done it—and it would have hurt Flip if he knew—but we needed the money. Flip was itching to use again, and we were talking about splitting town and starting over, someplace where we didn't know anybody.

"Technically, I was still married to Vaarni—on paper—so we stopped off in Nuevo Laredo to get divorced. But while I was at the courthouse Flip freaked out and bought tar from some creep he met in the cantina. So he was all fucked up when I got back with the papers. Well, he told me he didn't have any more, but he did—he tried to hide it in his backpack—and they nabbed him at the border. So I got stuck in Laredo with no money and no place to stay—and I don't have to tell you that was no picnic. The state took Tommy away and put him in a foster home, forchristsakes. I got him back, but it took me six weeks. I had to jump through a whole bunch of hoops—see a counselor, join a church, get a job, that kinda stuff. When Flip got out of jail we caught the first bus to Albuquerque and got married. Then we headed out to California to start over.

"But when Flip got busted they took away all his pills, and when he got to jail he didn't say anything about needing medication. He didn't tell anybody. He just quit taking it. I didn't notice, not at first. But after a while Flip stopped being himself—he got quiet, withdrawn. He took to talking to himself, and laughing in this little high-pitched tee-hee-hee, which I guess he thought only he could hear. Every time I asked him, 'What's so funny?' he'd say, 'I'm not laughing.'

"It isn't something you'd think about, you know, because he'd been doing so good—except for the little incident in Nuevo Laredo—and I had never seen him have a breakdown. I just knew about it in a vague kind of way. But I remembered that one night, after he told me he was clean, I asked him why he took pills every morning, and he told me they were mood elevators and they didn't really do anything except moderate his thinking 'cause he got crazy without them. And then he told me that he had flipped out in class one day—that was why they called him Flip—and he started throwing things and yelling and screaming at people that weren't there. 'It's hard to explain,' he said. 'But when I had these thoughts, or heard voices and such, my brain couldn't tell the difference between what it was thinking and what was real.'

"They sent him to the looney bin and put him on medication. He got better and they let him out. But after he got better he thought he didn't need the medication anymore, so he quit taking it. That was the first time he tried to kill himself. He jumped off a bridge, but they fished him out before he drowned."

April took a drag off the joint, but it had burned out. She felt around in her jeans for the lighter.

"There," I said, pointing down by her foot.

She picked it up and lit the joint, took a deep drag and held her breath. When she finally exhaled she said, "This is some good shit but it's green, wet. I got it from an old friend of Vaarni's in Humbolt. He he's got acres of the stuff. His family's Mexican—I mean really old Mexican. Before the Anglos came west they were settled there. So the cops leave him alone. Either that, or he pays them off. Where was I?"

"You were telling me about the canoe."

"Oh, yeah. So me and Flip and Tommy drove out to Yosemite for our honeymoon, and Flip stole this canoe in Merced so we could go rafting. It seemed like the trip was going to be a good thing. It calmed his nerves. For a few days, he was just like the old Flip again, quiet and shy, caring and kind. I was thinking maybe he didn't need the medication after all.

"You can only raft so far down the river because of the falls. They have a cable strung across the water and a sign that says: IF YOU GO IN THE WATER, YOU WILL DIE. Well, the last night we landed there, right there by the sign. I built a campfire, and I was about to cook supper when, out of the blue, Flip said, 'They're here,' and I looked around and said 'Who?' thinking maybe he meant the park rangers or something. And he said, 'Oh, it's nothing.' And the next thing I knew, he hopped into the canoe and headed for the falls.

"I shouted after him, but he didn't seem to hear. I ran down the bank screaming, but he didn't say a word. He looked at me, and smiled, and then he threw the paddle away. There was nothing anybody could do. He ducked under the cable and laid down in the canoe, and as God is my witness, I could hear him laughing. And then he was gone. They never did find the body. Flip would have liked that. He would say, 'Of course not—I told you they were here!' The rangers said they would likely find it in the summer under a snag when the runoff went down. And that," April said, standing up and arching her back, "was how I lost my second husband. Sad, isn't it?"

The joint had burned out and April lit it again, took a big hit, and then got up and crushed it out on the hearth. "So now you know why I do all this stuff."

"What stuff?"

"All this dope and drinking and shit."

"I don't know," I said, shaking my head. "I don't understand at all."

April tried standing on one leg in the middle of the room. She spread out her arms like wings, tilted her head back, and then brought her right index finger to her face and touched her nose. The she threw her arms out and stepped forward and said, "Ta Da! I practice my field sobriety tests all the time so I can pass them when the cops stop me."

"Do you get stopped often?" I asked.

"All the time. I fucked a state trooper last week outside of Olympia just for the hell of it."

I didn't say anything and after a minute April went limp and collapsed onto my shoulder sobbing. "I don't know," she said. "I don't know why I do half the stuff I do. I don't know why I liked Flip, or Vaarni, or any of them. They were all assholes. None of them loved me half as good as you did. I don't know why I ever left."

April's sobs turned to kisses and soon we were liplocked on the couch. "It's not a good time for me right now," she said. "Do you have any condoms?"

I said that I did, but when I got back she was out like a light. I wrapped her up in a blanket and left her on the couch. The next morning, when I got up, she was still there, and she didn't budge, even when I kissed her goodbye. I left two twenties on the counter with a note to buy herself and Tommy some lunch. When I got home from work she was gone. A few minutes later I heard the VW chugging up the drive. Then I heard Tommy playing in the yard with Newton and April came in with an armload of groceries. "Can I cook for you tonight?" she asked. "It's the least I can do."

And that was how it started. April put Tommy in school and he was pretty good about going. He made April solemnly swear (on the yellow pages) that she would look after Newton every day while he was gone. In the mornings, if April got him ready in time, he would walk down to the highway to catch the school bus, and I would see him and wave on my way to work. If not, I would drop him off, even though it wasn't on my way and made me late sometimes.

Dean-o didn't mind. He seemed happy for me, and the guys said something good had come over me. But if you asked me, I would have said that what changed was that I had what I was supposed to have had from the beginning. And one morning when I got up, and April was sleeping off her wine, and it was just me and Tommy making breakfast and packing our lunch, I stopped in front of the mirror on my way out the door.

I do have a big head, and my face is round, but it's big in a friendly way, or so I always thought. And my nose is crooked, and my ears are little, and they stick out. I have some gray in my whiskers, but my hair is still thick and black—that's the Indian in me—and I've got crow's feet around my eyes. I might not be the best-looking guy that ever lived, but I never did anybody any harm on purpose. I felt like a daddy. And when I stopped in front of the mirror and combed my hair, Tommy stopped with me and combed his hair, tried to part it the same way as mine, even though his hair is red and curly and wants to stick out all over. And when we went outside there was a note stuck under my windshield wiper that read, *Meet me at Boondock's on your way home.* I knew who it was from.

I had a bad feeling about things. I couldn't keep my mind on the job. I left work an hour early telling Dean-o I didn't feel well. I didn't wait long at the tavern, either. I high-tailed it out of there thinking I shouldn't have gone to work at all. I got home and the VW was gone. It looked like they'd left in a hurry, too. There were dishes in the sink and clothes in the washer. Newton was tied up on the back porch. When I let him loose he went straight to Tommy's room, and then room to room through the house, until finally he came back and sat down beside me and laid his head on his paws.

After a while I heard a car in the drive and I crept around the side of the garage and hung back until Jake got out and headed for the front door. A rage boiled up inside me. I don't lose my temper much, but I was on Jake before he was halfway to the porch. He didn't try to fight me. I clipped him in the jaw once, maybe twice, and then he was on his back and I was on top of him with my hands knotted around his neck. He didn't flinch. Newton brought me to my senses running around all excited and barking and biting me on the hand, his baby teeth like needles.

I got off Jake and he laid on the ground holding his throat, gasping for air. I stood over him and sucked the blood off my knuckles. "I don't blame you at all," he said. "Not one bit. I'd a done the same thing myself, if I was you."

Newton barked and ran back and forth nipping first at Jake's ear and then at my foot. Jake finally corralled him and sat up, scratching Newton behind the ears and rubbing his belly until he quieted down. "Cute little guy, ain't he?"

"Are you alright?" I asked.

Jake felt his jaw. "You got some powder in the keg," he said. "I got a tooth loose."

"Can I get you some ice?"

"I'll be alright. How 'bout a beer?"

"Sure," I said. "What the hell."

We sat on the porch. The sun was setting. Jake lit a cigarette. After a while he said, "I came by to tell you face-to-face what happened, and to thank you."

"For what?"

"For keeping April around until I could get a court order. You're a man of your word and I appreciate that."

"To tell you the truth, I'd forgot about it. I was hoping you'd gone back to Oklahoma."

"Oh, no," Jake said, shaking his head. "I can't give up. That boy's my flesh and blood, and I'd give everything I got to give him a good home."

"He had a good home."

"Yes, sir, and I appreciate that. I sure do. But I'm sure you can appreciate my predicament."

"He's not your son, Jake."

"Well, I say he is, and I aim to find out. You can't fault a fella for trying, now can you?"

I took a long pull off my beer. It was almost dark. The moon was just peeking over the eastern horizon. There was still a line of pink to the west, and it tinted the edge of the moon red. A crow cawed and I could see its silhouette pass by in the distance. Just behind it flew a larger bird, a hawk, maybe, or an owl, and it landed high in a tall pine. I could see the branch sway where it perched.

"Anyhow," Jake said, "I got a lawyer down in Bozeman, and he got a court order for the test. The sheriff come out this morning and served papers. She was supposed to take Tommy over to Sulphur Springs to draw blood. But April sweet-talked the cop into letting her shower and clean up—on her solemn promise to drive straight over—no doubt. But of course, she never showed. I reckon she's half-way to Canada by now." He sighed. "Anyhow, I wanted to tell you myself. No hard feelings?" Jake said, extending his hand.

I shook it without much enthusiasm and Jake gave Newton one final scratch and then stood up to go. "By the way, did she ever tell you about the canoe?"

"Yeah."

"Which version?"

"What do you mean...which version?"

"I mean which version. Was it the poor old Vietnam Vet who got shot down over Hanoi and spent seven years in a tiger cage? Or was it the tank commander from Desert Storm who breathed too much toxic dirt in Iraq? Or maybe it was the one about the poor kid who was abused by his daddy and never got straightened out?"

"That sounds more like it," I said. "It was more along those lines."

"I don't want to hurt your feelings or nothing, but that story was a lie. She made the whole thing up."

"Then what is the truth?" I asked—as if Jake would really know, or tell me if he did.

"Truth is she substituted some other pills for the ones he was supposed to take. He didn't know the difference. She just kept throwing out his prescription and giving him something else until nature ran its course."

"And you believe that?"

"It's a fact."

"Why would she do that? April might be a lot of things, but cold-blooded murderer ain't one of them."

Jake scratched his face and looked back over his shoulder at the moon. "She did it for the money."

"What money? She doesn't have any money."

"He had an inheritance. Oil money, or something like that."

"I thought you had all the money."

Jake laughed. "Me? Did she tell you that?"

I shrugged my shoulders.

"All that money and I'm staying at the Motel Six, except when I'm sleeping in my truck. And look at it. Why, it must have cost me five hundred dollars. I'm just floured in thousand dollar bills."

"I don't know what to believe anymore," I said. "I think you're both crazy."

"Some things you know," Jake said, "and others you take on faith. Do you know what the Bible says about faith, Frank?"

"What does the Bible say about faith, Jake?"

"The Bible says that faith is the assured expectation of things hoped for, the evident demonstration of reality, though not beheld. I walk by faith, Frank, not by sight."

"Like believing that Tommy's your son, even though he don't look anything like you?"

"He takes after my mother's side of the family."

"You're fucking crazy, you know. I should have blown you to hell the first night you set foot on my property."

"Now why would you want do that?"

"Because you're nuts, Jake, following April all over the country. There's laws against that kind of stuff. It's called stalking. You got her scared half to death."

"Would you say a man was crazy to follow a woman he thought stole his son, a woman who drank and did drugs and God-knows-what-all? A woman who might—just might, mind you—have murdered an innocent man? Would that make me crazy, Frank? To try to get my son away from such a woman?

"How 'bout this, Frank, what would you say if I told you I knew a man who pined away ten years for a woman who ran off with a guy who read meters for the electric company? What would you say if I told you he threw away the best part of his life waiting for a faithless woman who couldn't say no to a man? A woman who didn't have the decency to leave a note and say good bye. And after he waited ten years she came back with somebody else's kid and he took her in like she had never left. What would you say about that man, Frank? Would you say that he was crazy? Look at me, Frank. What would you say?"

"It was the gas company," I said.

"Come again?"

"It was the gas company. He read the meter for the gas company."

Jake walked back to his truck. "Think about it, Frank," he said. Then he drove away, to Canada, I suppose.

* * *

The snow held off for the longest time, but the weekend before Thanksgiving it hit hard. It blew sideways for forty-eight hours and piled up on the back porch so deep I couldn't open the door. I let Newton out to pee Friday and he never came back. I stood out front and called his name for hours, like to froze to death looking, but I never found him. Saturday morning I couldn't see to the end of the drive, and I could barely hear myself shout over the wind.

I stood on the porch Monday morning with a bottle of beer and understood what April meant when she said she drank so she didn't have to feel. The snow drifted half as high as the roof, but there were streaks of blue opening up through the clouds, and only a few flakes floated down. It was no use thinking about work—the highway wouldn't get plowed until Tuesday or Wednesday, and even if I went in, nobody else would show up. Thursday was Thanksgiving, and I'd have Friday off, as well. April had bought a fifteen-pound turkey and two bags of stuffing, sweet potatoes, a frozen cherry pie, dinner rolls, and a carton of ice cream. At least I'd eat. I don't know if they celebrate Thanksgiving in Canada, but I'd hate to think of April drinking wine under a bridge, alone, or Tommy sleeping in the van.

I thought about Flip, and wondered if there was such a man, and what he was really like, and if they would find his body in the summer when the water was low, the same way as I would find Newton when it thawed this spring. April said Flip couldn't tell the difference between what he was thinking and what was real, and I wondered if that was what people said about me. But what would happen if I lost faith? A vision crossed my mind of me laying down in a canoe, looking up at the sky, laughing as I floated over the falls. I shivered and went inside, shut the door and kicked the snow off my boots. She'll come back, I thought. Someday. I could hear Helen telling me the same thing. I suppose that's why I wait. Somebody's got to do it, and sometimes I'm all we got.

The End of the World

Walt Callaghan used to think that his son's troubles began when Shel, Walt's wife and Robbie's mother,died. But now that Robbie's gone, too, and Walt has what seems like all the time in the world, he's begun call to mind little things he and Shel didn't pay attention to way back when; things that didn't seem like much at the time but which, in retrospect, might have been important. Sometimes he wonders if all this would have happened no matter what, or if there was something he could have done differently—something that might have saved his son's life. And it's six in the evening and Walt stands on the balcony of his hotel room near the railway terminal in New Delhi, India, and the sun is setting, the sky illuminated in glowing curtains of orange and pink, and across the crooked and crowded little alley winding through the Paharganj Bazaar, even the white spires of the Shiva Temple have turned a deep shade of, dare he say, bloody red? Walt knows that it's the pollution that makes the sunset so colorful, but even so, it is pretty. And down the road Walt can hear the muezzin calling the Muslim faithful to prayer, and even this high-pitched, melodic, nasal incantation strikes Walt as both sweet and sad, the perfect benediction for a troubled day.

Walt has seen plenty of sunsets, but the last time he saw one this surreal he was hauling a load of ball-bearings from Kalamazoo to Seattle, and he was on I-90 out in the middle of Montana, and it was Sunday evening the 18th of May, 1980, and the date is fixed in Walt's mind for two reasons. The first is that Mount St. Helens blew that morning, and ash was falling even in Montana, a thousand miles away, and the resulting sunset was the most stunning Walt would see until this one in New Delhi. And the other is that when Walt called home that night to check in with Shel, he learned that Robbie had been born that morning, six weeks premature.

There were lots of deformed children in India. The hotel manager in Bombay warned Walt that women rented babies so they would look more pathetic when they begged. "Beggars," he said, his tone smug and accent slightly British, "sometimes maim their children." Walt thought this was nonsense. How could a parent do that to a child? But a few days later Walt saw a crowd of women fighting over a baby—a real tug-of-war with the child for a rope—and sure enough, the woman who emerged from the melee with the babe in her arms rushed to Walt and gestured to him that the child was hungry, and Walt turned away, disgusted.

But Robbie was not deformed, just premature. And though the insurance paid for the bulk of Robbie's forty-day stay in intensive care (almost $50,000), Walt's share still set them back $9,000, not counting time off from work. It took Walt nearly three years to pay it off, but that's what fatherhood is all about, isn't it? A man has to provide for his family. And when Walt deplaned in Bombay and walked around, he was shocked to see to what extent men and women went to care for their families. And then again, they sometimes maimed their children.

On the street below Walt watches a crowd of Muslims gathering in front of the mosque. His friends warned Walt to be careful in India, but the Muslims he'd met didn't seem dangerous. They were generally honest and clean, friendly and hard-working. Though Walt might not share their beliefs, they certainly weren't maiming their children. Not outwardly, anyway. And though Walt had been reluctant, at first, to disclose to them that he was an American (he hated lies, even "little white lies"), when he told them, he found that they were as eager to tell him that most Muslims didn't hate Americans as he was to tell them that most Americans didn't hate Muslims. Some interesting conversations followed, usually over tiny cups of strong, black coffee.

Watching all these fathers and sons walking into and out of the mosque reminded Walt of the time he came home and learned that Robbie had joined the Methodist Youth Foundation. Walt didn't believe in God and didn't think much of religion in general. His parents had been Southern Baptists and shoved enough religion down his throat to last two or three lifetimes. Shel was a lapsed Catholic. Walt had been on the road for nearly a month, and that night, after making it up to Shel in bed, she told him about Robbie's sudden interest in church. She said figured that it was all about a girl and it would pass, and sure enough, a girl turned up; though which came first, the youth group or the girl, Walt never found out. But the question nagged at Walt, What moved to Robbie try religion? For a while Walt had figured this was the beginning of Robbie's troubles, a non-descript group of clean-living kids who met on Wednesday nights to play Bible games, and on Saturday nights for pizza and a movie. Hell, there were parents around who'd be downright delighted if their kid signed up for a church group.

But on the plane to India, to claim what was left of Robbie's body, Walt remembered another time when he came home, and Robbie was maybe ten, and Walt had been on the road to God-knows-where, and it was two o'clock in the morning and Robbie was up late—he was always insomniac—and he was watching Sean Connery and Michael Caine in *The Man Who Would Be King* and Robbie looked up and said, matter-of-factly, "I'm going to Katmandu someday."

Walt paused at the door and wondered, What brought that on?

This was not long after Walt and Shel bought their first house: a 1950's post-war rambler, one of those "little boxes made of ticky-tacky" that "all looked just the same." And it was pink, when they bought it (though Walt painted it white right after they moved in), and the living room was square and plain, with green flower-print wallpaper, and a few pictures of the family hung about for show, and a hand-me-down sofa and loveseat combo Shel's parents gave them for a wedding present. And it was winter and snowing like all hell outside, and Walt had just come down from Wyoming with a load of feed, and the house had a cranky old oil furnace that put out about zero heat, and Robbie was wearing his favorite red and white *Speed Racer* PJ's, shivering in front of the TV.

"And when I was your age," Walt said, "I wanted to fly to the moon." And he scooped Robbie up and tucked him into bed.

On impulse Walt took out his *Lonely Planet* guide and found Katmandu on the map. It was almost exactly half-way around the world from Salt Lake City. Could Robbie have known that way back then? Walt wondered. Why Katmandu? Did he want even then to run as far away from us as he could?

The sun dipped alongside the spires of the Shiva Temple and seemed to grow in size as it approached the horizon. Walt had heard about the lens effect the atmosphere had—a kind of distortion that makes the sun or moon look bigger close to earth than overhead. But the sun, at least, was bigger than the earth, probably bigger than one could imagine without seeing it up close. So what kind of distortion was it, Walt wondered, if it showed the true nature of things more clearly?

Walt only meant to stay in New Delhi for a few days, just enough to take a break from the road. He'd flown from Salt Lake to Los Angeles, then to Hong Kong, Bangkok, and Bombay in one monumental long haul. Not that Walt hadn't made some long hauls in his day—San Francisco to New Orleans in fifty-eight hours with only one quick snooze and one speeding ticket. Salt Lake City to Casper Wyoming to Spokane Washington to Portland Oregon and home again. He'd have to count the hours from that trip on a calculator. But this was different. In those days Walt was young and muscular, his body supple, his engine always revved. He was ready to fight or fuck at the drop of a hat. And when the coffee quit working he could always buy pep pills in the shadowy corners of the truck stops.

But now Walt is nearing retirement age and feels it. His back is crooked and his hips are shot, he's got arthritis in his right wrist and elbow from jamming gears, and in his ankles from stomping the pedals. And his hearing's gone, too. On the flight from LA to Hong Kong they shoehorned the passengers in so tight, they couldn't have been closer if they were bunched like green bananas. By the time he reached Bombay, he was beat, and he slept for sixteen hours.

Walt came to India to claim Robbie's remains. But what do you do with the bones of your son, especially when he dedicated his life to putting as much distance between the two of you as he could? It was one thing to say good bye to Robbie. It was another to learn how to live with yourself. That first night in India, while Walt was sleeping, he dreamed that he and Robbie were on the road together in Walt's old Peterbilt. And when he woke up, Walt remembered that though Robbie had often asked, especially when he was younger, and Walt had promised many times, Walt never took Robbie on the road.

There were always reasons. For one, the trips were unpredictable, even dangerous. Walt might start out with a load to Denver expecting a return haul to Salt Lake City, but find when he arrived find that the return load had been yanked by another trucker, and all Walt had was a load to Tampa, or Des Moines, or Dallas, or wherever. There were hijackers, too, but they were rare, though not rare enough that Walt didn't pack a shotgun behind the seat and a chrome-plated .357 in the glove box. More likely were accidents, either on the road, or loading or unloading. And though Robbie asked to come along, he didn't understand—couldn't understand—what the road was really like. The days were long and the nights uncomfortable, either sacked out in the sleeper or checked into some fleabag truckstop hotel room. There were hours of mindless tedium.

They might be sitting in traffic in New Jersey, or stuck behind a landslide in Colorado, or maybe just driving across Kansas ("tell me that won't bore the balls off a brass monkey," Walt said). It wasn't kid-stuff, like a family lark to Disneyland. There was no TV, no time to run around and play tourist. It was Walt's job.

Walt took the train from Bombay to Gandhinigar to claim the body. He met with a deputy police inspector, Mr. Singh. Walt wanted to see the place, the "ashram," they called it, but Mr. Singh said that was "not possible." There was no explanation as to why. He showed Walt a backpack and some clothes. Walt nodded. They could have been Robbie's. Did it matter? Two policemen drove Walt to the coroner's office, a cubbyhole in a run-down warehouse in the middle of an industrial zone dedicated to baking bricks. A middle-aged man, the coroner, read the paperwork, gave Walt more papers to sign, and then handed Walt a large black briefcase—a briefcase. Walt shook it incredulously and heard what sounded like gravel inside. And when the man asked Walt how he wanted to dispose of the remains, Walt said he didn't know. Most people in India cremate their dead, the coroner explained. There were some churches with graveyards, though, for Christians, and he could direct Walt to one if Walt wanted. Walt said, "No thank you." Later that night, sitting alone in the dark in his hotel room, staring at the briefcase, Walt thought again about Robbie saying, "Someday I'm going to Katmandu." As far as he knew, Robbie never got there.

The next morning Walt went to the train station and found a rail map of India. He fought the crowds to the ticket line and exchanged his return ticket to Bombay for a ticket to Jaipur. From Jaipur he'd gone to Agra (can't come to India and not see the Taj), then Delhi, to rest up for a few days, and, finally, he had a ticket across India to Gorukpur. There Walt would catch a bus north, to the Nepal border, and then on to Katmandu.

But in Delhi Walt got sick—a fever, diarrhea, cramps the worst he'd ever had. He was in no condition to travel. He practically crawled through the bazaar to a one-room office where a man calling himself Dr. Pahar ran a clinic. And though Dr. Pahar didn't speak a word of English, and Walt didn't speak a word of Hindi, Walt managed to communicate enough that the doctor prescribed him six doses of five pills (one orange, two white, and two green) three times a day for two days. Walt didn't ask what they were, but damned if the first night the fever didn't break. And now, on the evening of the second day, Walt felt well enough to push on.

Robbie had been good at pushing on. After the youth-group debacle (which ended when the girl's parents caught them having "phone sex" and ordered Shel to keep Robbie away from their daughter), Robbie seemed to lose interest in religion. But the interest that surfaced after was worse.

Walt laughed his first night in Delhi. The street touts bombarded him with offers of hashish and marijuana and opium. And Walt saw disheveled knots of vagrants squatting on corners in broad daylight holding lighters under makeshift tinfoil cookers and smoking heroin. It wasn't like Walt hadn't sewn his wild oats. But there comes a time when you have to be a man about things. You do your job. And when drugs got in the way of Walt's life, and Shel, then his girlfriend, put her foot down, Walt cleaned up his act. He never touched them again. Except, of course, in a professional capacity.

Walt shouldered Robbie's backpack.

At the police station in Gugarat, the meticulous Inspector Singh had itemized everything and provided Walt with a receipt which he insisted Walt sign, despite the fact that it was written in Hindi and Walt couldn't read a word of it. After he picked up Robbie's bones, and went back to the hotel, Walt sat down on his bed. It was five-thirty in the afternoon. He opened the backpack and slowly emptied it. No doubt, it was the authorities who folded the clothes so carefully and packed them so neatly. Robbie would never do that.

Walt checked the pockets. He was reasonably sure the police had been through them already, but you never knew. And he wasn't sure what Robbie might have left behind. What do you carry in your pockets on the day you commit suicide? There was a battered shaving kit Walt recognized as one he gave Robbie for Christmas years ago. And sandals, clothes—all Indian, none western (except for three pair of white cotton briefs)—beads, books (in Hindi, mostly, along with an English/Hindi dictionary, and a few English titles touting "The Way of the Lotus" and "The Mystery of Life Unfolded" by Swami Chittrya Varma, and a plain, navy blue woolen shawl big enough to have doubled as a blanket. Walt held a shirt up and tried to imagine Robbie wearing it. It was simple enough, long sleeved, hanging to the knee, made from plain, undyed cotton. The drawstring pajama pants were of similar material. At the bottom of the shaving kit was a thin black cord with two silver charms hanging on it. Walt remembered Robbie wearing the charms home from his first trip to India and explaining that one was the elephant-headed God, Ganesh, who was supposed to safe-guard travelers, and the other was Ma Kali, brandishing her sword and wearing a necklace of severed heads and a skirt of severed arms. She was, Robbie said, supposed to ward away evil.

Some good these did, Walt thought.

Robbie's first trip to India ended in a bout of meningitis that nearly killed him. From what Walt could gather, after Robbie was strong enough to come home to recuperate, was that Robbie spent most of his time wandering the beaches of Goa in a drug-induced stupor with a crowd of hip young foreigners. They drank and drugged and slept around, and God-only-knows how they all kept from dying, what with all the filth and disease Walt had seen since he came to India to see for himself.

Robbie's recovery took six months, but as life returned to his body, it seemed to fade from his spirit. When Walt got up to go to work on Monday morning, Robbie was sitting at the kitchen table. And when Walt came home on Wednesday evening Robbie was still there, sometimes wearing the same clothes. If Walt pointed out Robbie's slovenliness, Robbie shrugged his shoulders and said, "They're just clothes." And then one day Walt came home and Robbie was gone. A note on the table said, "Time to move on."

What followed were two years of one-way correspondence beginning with a postcard from Kingman Arizona announcing that Robbie had done a sun ceremony and a vision quest complete with peyote. And then there was a letter from a monastery in Italy accessible only by boat, and another postcard, blank, from an island off the coast of Greece, showing an impossibly steep cliff rising from the sea, with a set of crooked steps hewn from the stone leading to a round white spire perched precariously at the very top. And there was a letter from the military commander of some district in Serbia advising Walt that Robbie had been detained trying to enter the country illegally, but another letter arrived the next day postmarked Sarajevo saying that Robbie was okay, but that there was a scam going on where border guards took down passport information and wrote bogus letters home advising families that that their children had been arrested in order to extort "fines" from them. And there was a letter from a UN Peacekeeper from Belgium with a picture and note to Robbie (in English) that said he missed him and hoped Robbie was okay. And there was a letter from Egypt saying that Robbie was going to try to sneak in to Mecca for the Haj, and then a card from Thailand, and one from Bali, and another from Fiji telling Walt that there were still cannibals on the island, though it was considered bad form to practice on tourists. And then there was a long period of silence followed, at length, by a letter in which Robbie said he had joined an Ashram in Gugarat, in the high desert, and had renounced material possessions, but in doing so, had found inner peace. In the letter was a page torn from a Bible—the Book of Ecclesiastes—and highlighted on the page was a line: everything is vanity.

At the bottom of Robbie's pack was an old Bible, and when Walt opened it to Ecclesiastes, sure enough, a page was missing. But in its place was a note, in Robbie's neat handwriting that read, "There is a pattern in all things. Someday, Dad, I hope that you understand."

Walt was stunned. He walked to the balcony with the note and read it again, went back into the room and turned the Bible upside down, flipped the pages through to see if there were any more notes. There weren't. He folded the note and put it in his wallet and went out to get a bite of supper. In the middle of the night he woke up, took the note out and read it again. That was when Walt decided to throw away his old Samsonite and take Robbie's backpack and hit the road to Katmandu.

In the morning Walt went through the rest of Robbie's stuff, finding nothing interesting except the Ganesh and Kali charms. He held these in his hand for a moment before tossing them in the suitcase, along with all the rest of the things that wouldn't fit in the backpack. He carried the suitcase downstairs and out to the street. Walt knew some poor bastard would haul it off as soon as Walt's back was turned. But when he laid the suitcase down he hesitated, then opened it and took out the charms and looked at them again. They weren't worth much, but Robbie didn't leave much behind for Walt to remember him by. Walt hung them around his neck.

* * *

Walt paid his bill, then forced his way through the crowd in the bazaar the half mile or so to the train station. He inquired at the ticket window and was told the train to Gorukpur departed from platform ten. Walt checked his watch. It was seven-thirty. The train left at ten past eight. Plenty of time. Walt found the stairway to the overpass and made his way through the mass of outward (and downward) bound passengers to the bridge that spanned the tracks and linked the individual platforms.

There were twelve platforms. Ten was at the far end.

Walt struggled with the backpack and the briefcase. He could not imagine what drove Indians to behave as they did when it came to order and lines. Pay three rupees for an envelope and a clerk will duly record the transaction in a ledger in triplicate and then record it again in a receipt book for the customer. But ask him to line up in a queue, or even to drive in one lane on the highway, and he'll look at you like you're crazy. In theory, they drove on the left side of the road, but that was negotiable, at best, depending on how much and what kind of traffic was in the oncoming lane. And now Walt was trying to jam his way through the overpass with his son's bones in a briefcase and a fat backpack weighing down on his bad back, and he cursed the insanity.

When he reached the tenth platform Walt descended the stairs and began searching for the Second A/C rail cars. He walked all the way to the engine without finding one, then backtracked and found two near the end of the train. He scanned the seating assignments posted by the doors and could not find his name. He asked a conductor, "Is this the train to Gorukpur?" The conductor wobbled his head from side-to-side, which in India could mean either yes or no.

"I can't find my seat assignment," Walt said.

The conductor asked for his ticket, read it, then examined the passenger lists. He pointed to a blank line by a seat assignment. "Yours," he said.

But then Walt noticed that his ticket was for train 2556, and the manifest was for train 2554. Maybe there was no difference. It might be 2556 in one direction, 2554 in the other, but Walt wasn't one to leave things to chance. He asked a platform manager, and he replied that the train to Gorukpur was on platform twelve. Walt checked his watch. It was five minutes to eight. Okay, he thought, good job I got here early. Plenty of time.

He plowed his way up the stairway (Wasn't anybody but him going upstairs? Where did all these people come from?). Platform twelve was a hop and skip down the bridge, and Walt battled his way down the stairs and followed the train in the other direction and found the engine at that end, but no second A/C car. Now he was sweating. There were no assignments posted on the lower class cars, people just piled in until no more could fit, and then a few more crammed in after them. Walt wondered if the logic behind placing the first and second class cars at the end of the train was a holdover from the days of the wood and coal burning engines: less smoke. Just like India, Walt thought, always been that way, always be that way.

He back-tracked the length of the train and found the second class cars, and to his dismay, they were for a train number 6650. God only knew where it went. Walt might have climbed on and woke up in the morning in Afghanistan. He paused and laughed out loud. Robbie would have loved that. People stared. Walt checked his watch. Eight o'clock. He asked another platform manager. The man demanded Walt's ticket. Walt handed it over. The man scrutinized it. "Platform eight," he said. He handed Walt the ticket and disappeared into the crowd.

Walt leaned forward to take the weight of the pack off his shoulders. 6650, wherever it went, was about to depart, and the platform was packed with well-wishers seeing loved ones off. Walt bulled his way to the stairway and up, then back down the overpass to platform eight. They can't have two trains leaving in the same direction at the same time, he reasoned, and if the engine on this one faces one way...but then Walt stopped and asked himself, what would Robbie do? Instead of heading in the logical direction, he headed in the same direction as before, found his car, his seat assignment, and climbed on just as the train pulled out. Where but in India? Walt wondered.

There was only one other passenger in the car, and that was how Walt met Simeone.

Simeone was taller than Walt, and much younger, twenty or twenty-one, he guessed; willow-thin, and slightly red-faced, as though she was constantly blushing. She had disheveled honey-blonde hair roughly cut above her shoulders, and a careless way about her that suggested she had been on the road for a while. But for all her ordinariness, there was something pretty about her; her lips, perhaps, which were plump, and seemed always on the verge of a smile; or her eyes, clear and blue, but with a hint of remote sadness. Their eyes met momentarily, and then Walt looked away.

Walt had been assigned an aisle berth, Simeone was in one of the four-wide berths on the opposite side. Walt jammed the backpack under his seat and nested the briefcase next to him before he stole a second look at Simeone. He glanced at her, turned away, then looked again, embarrassed that she had caught him staring. A minute later she took the seat opposite him. "You are an American," she said, her accent French.

"Yes," he replied.

She pulled out a tattered Lonely Planet and pointed to a map of Uttar Pradesh. "Do you know how many hours to this place?"

The lighting on the train was dim, and Walt held the book close to his face so he could see. He wasn't sure exactly where she was pointing.

"Where are you going?" she asked.

"Katmandu," he replied.

"Me too. Perhaps we can travel together."

Walt was stunned. He had been in India nearly two weeks and hadn't had a soul speak to him who wasn't expecting money. He looked at Simeone and she looked at him. Perhaps it was a good idea to partner up, to convoy, as he used to say.

He offered her his hand, "Walt Callaghan."

"Simeone Chenette."

"And what brings you to India?"

Simeone shrugged. "I'm traveling. And you?"

Walt paused. How do you explain to someone that you are carrying your son's bones to Katmandu? But he didn't like to lie, so he told her, "I'm taking my son's bones to Katmandu."

She nodded, as though it was an ordinary thing. "That is good," she said.

"Forgive me for asking," Walt said, "but aren't you afraid, traveling alone?"

"Not at all. I feel safer in India than I did in America. Besides, you know, you always meet the right people at the right time. If your karma is good." She paused, and looked at Walt. "Do you believe in karma?"

Here we go, Walt thought. "No, I'm not much on eastern religion, or any religion, for that matter."

"Karma is not about religion, and it doesn't care whether you believe or not. Karma is about knowing that what you put into life is what you will get out of it."

"I dunno. It seems like I put a lot into life without getting much in return."

"Then maybe you are not on the right path."

"I'm fifty-one years old, and you're telling me that I'm not on the right path?"

"I didn't tell you anything," Simeone said, laughing. "You said."

Walt scratched his head. He didn't remember saying.

The conductor came down the aisle and checked their tickets officiously. He pointed out that Simeone's seat assignment was on the other side of the aisle, then eyed her suspiciously as though he were worried she and Walt might be up to something. Walt suppressed a grin. Outside of a few truckstop girls, he hadn't been with a woman since Shel died. And even they weren't very satisfying. At some point Walt realized that what he wanted wasn't for sale, so what was the point? It had been years since he was with a woman. So what if Simeone was pretty? What would a girl like her see in him? But it would be funny to see the authorities make a fuss, if they did get together, and if they got caught. It would undoubtedly break more regulations than Walt could count. And then he remembered that Robbie once told him a story about making love to a girl on a Greyhound bus on one of his cross-country trips between Salt Lake and someplace.

"How could you do that?" Walt asked, "Have sex with a stranger? In public, no less."

"It's only sex," Robbie replied, "and she was willing enough."

Walt looked at Simeone and wondered if this was the kind of girl Robbie met.

"You see," Simeone said, "there is Karma and there is Dharma. Karma is the law that what you put into the world you get out of it. But Dharma is about knowing your place in the world. If you are not on the right path, it doesn't matter how much effort you put into it, you won't get where you want to go. But if you are in the right place, every good thing that you do helps you along the way. The path unfolds before you, effortlessly."

"And what is your place?" Walt asked.

Simeone laughed. "Me? I am so young, I am still learning that out."

"How old are you?"

"Twenty-three."

Simeone took the book from Walt and tucked it into a side pouch on her backpack. While she was occupied, the porter came down the aisle with sheets and blankets and pillows. Simeone folded her seat down and made her bed. Walt began to do the same. Simeone looked up and patted the lower berth opposite her. "You can sleep here if you want, it is more comfortable."

Now it was Walt's turn to blush, but to his surprise, he found himself saying, "Okay."

But nothing happened that night. Simeone made her bed and wrapped up in a blanket, and Walt wrapped up in his blanket, and in a few minutes she was snoring, and Walt lay wide awake thinking about Robbie.

* * *

Robbie was seventeen when Shel got sick. They weren't so progressive about breast cancer in those days, and by the time Shell said something about lumps it was too late for even a mastectomy, the cancer had spread to her lymph nodes, her bones, her brain. She wasted away, pale, thin, bruised. She acquired tremors, and eventually, full-blown seizures. She and Walt had agreed to keep it from Robbie, let him have as many happy, normal years in high school as possible. But the cancer progressed more rapidly than they anticipated, and one rare weekend when Walt was home, Robbie asked him out for lunch.

It was October, 1995, and the Cowboys were playing the Eagles, and the Cowboys were good that year and getting better. Interrupting Walt during a game was taboo—the blue star was as close to a religious icon as anything Walt avowed—but the Cowboys were down by thirteen and the first quarter wasn't halfway through, so Walt shut off the TV in disgust and drove Robbie to a truckstop on I-15. Robbie asked, "Is mom dying?"

Walt fumbled with his napkin.

"It's not like I don't have eyes, for christsake," Robbie said. Robbie was tall and willow-thin, blonde like his mom, with long, frizzy hair pulled back in a pony tail. He wore a diamond stud in left ear, a wispy line of peach fuzz over his lip. Only the day before Walt had a conniption fit when he saw Robbie without a shirt: he sported a Celtic tattoo on his right bicep and another of an Egyptian hieroglyphic on his left shoulder blade.

"You're too young for that shit," Walt said.

"It's just a tattoo," Robbie argued. "Everybody's getting them."

"And if everybody got their dicks cropped, would you do that, too?"

"You got one."

"I got two or three, but I wished I didn't. You can't wash 'em off when you get tired of 'em."

"It's the sign of Ra."

"Rah, rah, rah," Walt growled.

"The Sun God. Puh-leeze"

Walt said, "At least I got normal tattoos. And don't pul-leeze me."

37

"Okay, then, I'll get another one, and bigger." And later on, he did, making a point that Walt saw it, a curious, curvy thing like a face with a pair of heavily-lidded eyes and a nose like a convoluted question mark.

The waitress brought their burgers and Walt asked if she could turn on the TV behind the counter. The Cowboys were up by twenty-one. Walt swore under his breath.

Walt never asked where Robbie got the money for the tattoos or the diamond stud, or the designer clothes he wore. Robbie couldn't hold a steady job, though there was always some place he had to be. As Walt stared out the window watching India race past in the moonlight, he wondered if he didn't ask because in his heart he knew the answer, or because he knew Robbie could lie, could tell him anything, and he wouldn't know Robbie well enough to say otherwise.

"So why not just tell me and get it over with," Robbie said.

"Shel's dying," Walt replied. Then he burst into tears.

* * *

After Shel died, Walt and Robbie were little more than house-mates. Walt talked to Abe, his boss, about sticking closer to home, but there wasn't much the company could (or would) do. "I can't save every local haul for you," Abe said. "How would that be for my other drivers?" Walt tried for a while—even turned down some of the more profitable longer runs—but within a few months, it was business-as-usual. After a while, if anything, he drew even more long hauls than before. Home wasn't the same without Shel around.

Until then Robbie had been a decent student, A's and B's, but his junior year his grades plummeted to B's and C's, and his senior year he drew his first "D." Walt prodded Robbie about post-graduation plans. Robbie talked for a while about community college, maybe taking some computer classes at a tech school, or photography. One day Walt found a brochure in the mail from a fashion-design school in New York.

Robbie seemed to have a sixth sense about Walt's schedule. Walt knew Robbie had been home by the food gone missing from the refrigerator and the mess Robbie left behind, but their paths seldom crossed. They communicated via notes left by the coffee pot. Then one Monday afternoon Walt blew a transmission on his way to Albuquerque. He left the truck in a garage and hopped a bus back to Salt Lake. It was close to ten when the taxi dropped him out front. Robbie was home—at least, Shel's old car was parked in the drive. But there was another car parked there, too, a fancy new yellow mustang. Walt knocked softly on Robbie's door. He peeked inside. Robbie had company. No big deal. Walt done the same thing when he was Robbie's age. He presumed Robbie knew enough to use a condom. But then Robbie's partner sat up. Perhaps he slept lightly, being in a strange home and all. But there was no question about it, Robbie was sleeping with a boy.

Walt's face flushed and his ears began to ring. He closed the door and went into kitchen, cracked a beer. What should he do? His first inclination was to kill them both and be done with it. He could plead insanity. He might get away with it in Utah. He could claim he thought his son was being raped. The right jury might buy that.

He thought about Shel—she'd always dealt with this kind of stuff. What would she have done? He called Shel's face to mind, not sick, not dying, but younger, sitting in a bathrobe at two o'clock in the morning, the way she used to look when she was waiting for Walt to come home. "Hey, baby," Walt would say, bounding through the front door and gathering her in his arms. "How've you been?"

She would put up a mock struggle, shush Walt so he wouldn't wake Robbie, then take him by the hand and lead him to the bedroom. Afterwards she would say, "We got a little problem with Robbie," and she would lay the story out, but then wrap it up saying, "but don't worry, I got it under control."

Walt wondered what his buddies at work would say if they knew. Did you hear? Walt Callaghan's kid is a fudge-packer.

But was Robbie gay? Maybe this just an experiment, a phase he was going through? That's what Shel would say. Walt took a deep breath. He was off the hook.

Until a few years ago, he might have killed the boy, anyway, for coming into his house and sleeping with his son. But when Shel was dying, she and Walt had gone to see a naturopath, a last-grasp kind of a thing, and Dr. Weinstein had been very nice. He spend more time with Shel than all the other doctors put together, and even though he couldn't save her, his advice (strict vegetarian diet, homeopathic remedies) did ease her pain considerably. And when it came time to settle accounts, Dr. Weinstein told Walt to pay what he could and forget the rest. A few months after Shel died Walt saw Dr. Weinstein featured prominently on the front page of the

Salt Lake City Herald on "Come Out of the Closet Day." It was hard to hate a man who'd been so nice to you.

In the end, Walt hadn't had to make a decision. When he woke up in the morning Robbie was gone, and he wouldn't return until he was recovering from the meningitis that nearly killed him.

* * *

In the middle of the night Walt realized he had left the briefcase under his assigned seat. The train wasn't crowded, but even so... And the briefcase wasn't something he wanted stolen. He imagined a thief breaking it open. What Walt wouldn't give to see the look on his face then. Actually, Walt had no way of knowing what was inside. It could be gravel for all he knew. The day Walt picked up Robbie's remains, he'd been tempted to open it. He sat in his hotel room, on a chair facing the bed, with the briefcase in front of him. But in the end, he couldn't bring himself to do it. And even if it was bones, how could anyone know for sure whose bones they were? The Indians hadn't asked for DNA samples. And he doubted if the authorities would go to a lot of trouble and expense over one more dead foreigner. Most likely there was some kind of clue. In the end, Walt thought, Robbie would say it didn't matter. They're just bones. Still, he had bought a little brass lock to keep them safe. He got up and tucked the briefcase next to him in bed.

Walt slept, and when he got up, he was surprised to find what looked all the conductors on the train sleeping in the berths around him and Simeone. It was an odd sight, all these men in neat blue uniforms, sleeping.

Morning came. Simeone slept soundly. The train stopped and Walt hopped off briefly to get them a snack, but didn't like the look of the platform vendors. At least I have water, he thought, and they'll serve me breakfast on the train in a while. When he climbed back on board, he saw that the conductors had all purchased omelets. "Good thing you ate," one said. "With so few passengers, they didn't give us a pantry car." When Walt sat down he realized that while they were stopped, someone had come through and cleaned out the car. Walt's water bottle was gone.

Simeone woke up and stretched, lazy and feline. She smiled at Walt, and he thought she looked quite pretty. She went to the loo, came back, stripped down her bed, then took out a bag of trail mix from her pack and offered some to Walt.

* * *

In Gorukpur Walt found a travel agent who took money from them for bus tickets to Katmandu and promptly disappeared. Five minutes passed, then ten. They were sitting in a little storefront office—Walt didn't even know whether the man worked there or just smelled opportunity. The whole thing had the feeling of a dope deal gone bad, sitting in a car waiting for Jose. Simeone wasn't worried at all. Eventually the man came back and directed them to an SUV, where the driver took their backpacks and stashed them in a rack on top. He gestured for the briefcase. Walt clutched it to his chest. "This rides with me," he said.

They crammed fourteen people in a car made for eight and hit the road. Walt and Simeone had paid for front seat tickets, but so, apparently, had three other people, not including the driver. There was a lot of shouting and animated arm waving, and the driver and several of the passengers tried again to make Walt part with the briefcase, but he would not let it go. He could only imagine what they were thinking.

In the middle of the melee Simeone turned to Walt and said: "An American, a Frenchman, and an Indian were riding in airplane. After a while, the American got up and told the pilot to land, that they were flying over America. 'How can you tell?' the pilot asked. 'Because I opened the window and saw that you are flying over buildings so tall you are almost touching them.' The pilot laughed and landed the plane. They were in New York. A while later, the Frenchman got up and told the pilot, 'Stop the plane!' 'Why?' asked the pilot. 'Because you are flying over France.' 'But how can you tell?' 'Because when I opened the window I smelled the cooking.' The pilot landed the plane. They were in Paris. After a while, the Indian shouted, 'Stop the plane!' The pilot asked, 'Why?' 'Because we are in India.' 'How can you tell,' the pilot asked. 'Because when I opened the window, someone stole my watch.'"

Walt burst out laughing. The melee broke up and Walt and Simeone and a young Nepali crammed into the front seat. The Nepali straddled the stickshift, the bitch position, they used to call it when Walt was young and he and his friends sometimes rode four in the front of a pickup truck. After a while, he found it was more comfortable for all if he rode with his arm draped over Simeone's shoulder. She let her hand rest carelessly on his thigh.

Walt had been in India long enough that the traffic didn't frighten him anymore, but he hadn't yet been out on the open road. It felt nice, he thought, and even better to be a passenger for a change. He had no idea how many miles he'd logged in his lifetime, but he probably hadn't been a passenger more than ten days since he'd got his interstate combo license. Once, when Walt came home from making a couple of runs up and down the west coast, Robbie asked him what Walt thought of the Golden Gate Bridge. All Walt could remember was sweating in traffic. He couldn't even tell Robbie what color it was.

They rolled out of Gorukpur into a vast plain of rice paddies and safflower fields. The safflowers, especially, were beautiful; bright patch-work carpets of yellow and green stretching for miles, all the way to the feet of the mountains. Simeone was humming softly to herself. Walt was surprised to recognize the song: "Willing." When Simeone reached the refrain, Walt joined in, "I been from Tucson to Tucumcari, Tehachapi to Tonopah, I've driven every kind of rig that's ever been made..." Simeone seemed surprised that Walt knew the words. But he had been from Tucson to Tucumcari, many times, and Tehatachapie to Tonopah, too, and other roads as bad, even worse. Walt looked around. This, by God, was the damndest trip he'd ever made.

Walt had to hand it to the driver: the kid had balls. The road was bad, practically impassible. It had been paved once, by the British, Walt guessed, but like so many things in India, it looked like the maintenance stopped on Independence Day. But the driver honked and braked and swerved his way around ruts and potholes, shot past oxcarts and trucks and slower buses, practically forcing them off the road; always an eyelash away from disaster, but never quite getting there.

It was nearly six when they reached the Nepalese border at Sunoli. Walt knew there was trouble before they reached town. The road was lined with parked trucks—never a good sign. And sure enough, the border was closed. The driver put on another show. He waived his arms and shouted excitedly, and no doubt, his concern genuine. He got paid by the trip, and the delay would cost him money. A crowd of ragged-looking strangers swarmed over the car taking down the luggage. Walt tried to stop them, but there were too many. He settled for retrieving his and Simeone's backpacks.

The only other person in the car who spoke English was a young Nepali man returning from working in India. "What are they saying?"

Walt asked.

"They say there was a strike by the Maoists and the roads are closed."

"A strike?" Walt pictured a picket line slowly circling in front of factories and office buildings. "What about?"

"They are protesting the government."

Well, so be it, Walt thought. You had to expect stuff like this when you traveled. "What now?" he asked.

The man shrugged his shoulders. We can cross into Nepal, but there is no traffic allowed past the city. They say tomorrow the road will open."

Walt and Simeone took a rickshaw to the border. The Indians stamped their exit visas without comment. At the Nepali post they shelled out 1500 Indian rupees each for a visa. The guards were disinterested, their manner lackadaisical. Walt noted that while his wallet was bursting, he carried about 30,000 rupees, besides credit cards, Simeone had to sort through a tattered purse of crumpled old bills to scrounge the money. She was about busted.

Walt knew instinctively that rooms would be at a premium—truckstops lived for days like this when demand was high and supply low. He asked around until he found a rickshaw driver who said he knew where a room might still be had. The driver dropped them off in front of a building that looked like it had survived world war three. Or hadn't survived, might be a better description. There were no lights save candles. The front desk was behind a bar, and Walt immediately fingered the place for a whorehouse. The clerk said he had one room.

"Would you like to share?" Walt asked.

"Sure," Simeone replied.

Walt paid the man 500 Indian rupees and they followed a boy with a flashlight up a crooked set of stairs to a rooftop room so ratty Walt would have sworn it was a storage area had it not had fresh vomit stains on the floor and walls. There were two sagging beds with what looked like clean sheets (though Walt thought he would be more comfortable not knowing), thick Nepali quilts, and a squat toilet in an adjoining room with a door so warped it wouldn't close. Walt gave the boy a hundred rupee tip and the boy left the flashlight.

Walt and Simeone dropped their bags wearily and trudged through town in search of dinner. Later on, they stumped back up the stairs and Walt was taken aback to see Simeone strip down to her panties and climb into bed. It was dark, but not that dark. Oh, well, Walt thought, and he stripped down to his shorts and climbed into the other bed. In a minute Simeone asked, "Aren't you going to sleep with me?"

Walt froze. He was tired for one thing, and cold, and the combination of the two wasn't complimentary to the male anatomy. And sex hadn't been on his mind. But without waiting for a reply Simeone got up, climbed into Walt's bed, straddled him, and nature took its course. Walt fucked her good and hard for an hour, then after a few minutes to catch his breath, he fucked her again, just to make sure. And they fell asleep warm and sticky and sweaty and entwined in each others' arms.

That night Walt dreamed about Shel and when he woke up in the morning Simeone's head was nested on his shoulder, just like Shel used to do when he came in from the road. He gently disentangled himself and used the bathroom, and when he came back he stopped and looked as Simeone sleeping in the watery morning light. This is someone's daughter, Walt thought. Hell, she's young enough to be my daughter. But he didn't feel guilty. He had no unrealistic expectations. He knew that when they reached Katmandu, she would go her way, and he would go his, but he was glad for the moment they shared. It made the road less lonely, if only for a little while. And when he slipped back into bed beside her, he realized that she had, on her right shoulder blade, the same curious tattoo that Robbie had had on his.

Walt lay in bed softly stroking Simeone's hair. When she woke up, she kissed him on the mouth and they made love again before dressing and walking into town.

As Walt expected, the jeep was gone. The driver probably went back to Gorukpur the night before. But the road was lined with busses, and Walt figured one of them must go to Katmandu, and so he and Simeone walked down the road asking drivers until they found one willing to take them.

The drive was even prettier than the day before, the Nepali roads in better repair. Walt sank into his seat and took in the countryside. The valley was green and fertile, dotted with clusters of houses. The homes were often elevated above the fields on brick foundations, and Walt presumed that come monsoon the whole valley would be underwater. The people were poor—probably subsistence farmers—but despite the third world conditions there was a kind of charm to the scene, and Walt was struck by a thought that he could live there, if he wanted.

44

Whole families stood in front of their homes brushing their teeth. Mothers pumped water from wells by hand onto laughing, splashing children. Men squatted on their haunches smoking God-knows-what. In India, it seemed, anything that could be cut and dried was fair game to smoke: tobacco, ganja, camel-shit, or all three mixed together. And there were lines of women in colorful saris walking out into the countryside to tend their fields, and knots of school children in Catholic-style school uniforms dawdling along as children anywhere might on their way to school. Walt remembered a tout in Jaipur who explained that the Catholics had no interest in education, they just want to convert the Indians. And the Indians had no interest in converting, they just wanted a basic education. They system, he explained, tottered along to everyone's equal dissatisfaction, except that every now and then there was a student who converted, or more likely, a student who attached him or herself to a teacher long enough to learn something. So from time to time, the system did work. From time to time.

"Do you see?" Simeone said. "They have nothing, yet they are so happy."

"Until one of their children dies of a curable disease," Walt replied.

"But even that does not stop them. They say it is their fate."

"Then why bother with vaccines?" Walt asked.

"Even in America, children die. If it is your time, it is your time. You cannot struggle against it. I mean, you can, but why?"

"Do you have parents?" Walt asked.

"Of course I do," Simeone said, laughing.

"I mean, Are you close to them?"

"My mother lives in Nice, we are very close. My father is in the diplomatic corps. He is somewhere...Tunisia, I think. And you, do you have family? I mean, besides..."

"My wife died seven years ago."

"No parents?"

"They're gone, too."

"I am sorry."

The bus slowed to a halt and Walt looked out the window. He was surprised to see soldiers crouched behind a sandbag emplacement with a machine gun. He whistled through his teeth.

"There is a war going on," Simeone said. "The Maoists are trying to get rid of the king." And then Walt realized that when the Nepali boy said "strike," he was not talking about a bunch of good old boys standing around a burn barrel drinking coffee and waving picket signs, he meant an attack. And though Walt hadn't been to Vietnam, he had seen enough pictures of war to know when soldiers meant business, and these guys were for real.

The bus crawled forward. In a few minutes a tall, grim-faced soldier wearing a Kevlar vest and cradling an M-16 boarded the bus. He came down the aisle, scowling as he examined the passengers' faces. He paused and stared down at Walt, then he moved on. At the back of the bus he said something in Nepali. Everybody got up and reached for their bags, but when Walt stood up, one of the passengers patted him on the arm and said, "Not you. They are only interested in us."

The passengers disembarked, presumably to be searched and have their papers checked. The bus passed through the checkpoint and loaded them all back on again. They were passing a military facility. The passenger who had stopped Walt from getting off touched him lightly on the shoulder. "Last night, guerillas killed six soldiers here."

The base itself was heavily fortified with anti-infiltration concertina wire staked out in a wide pattern surrounding the perimeter. Probably mined, Walt thought. And every few yards there were gun emplacements or watchtowers, all sandbagged and alertly manned. And then Walt saw the damnedest thing he had ever seen, what was clearly a gallows, a scaffolding set up in the middle of a field. It wasn't for loading trucks—there was no road leading to it. Just a platform with a pipe bar erected over it from which hung a half-dozen ropes. Simeone took Walt's hand and squeezed it.

And then the bus picked up speed, and just as quickly they were winding their way through a pleasant countryside as though nothing at all unusual had happened. And this scene would be repeated twenty times in the 200 kilometers to Katmandu.

"Tell me about your tattoo," Walt said.

"Which one?"

"The one on your shoulder."

"It is called The Merciful Eyes of Vimochana, why?"

"My son had one like it."

Simeone smiled. "He must have been a good boy. The eyes are like the eyes of God that see in every direction. The dot is the third eye, the one that judges hearts. And this," she said, tracing a backwards question mark in the air with her finger, "is sometimes interpreted as the Nepali number one, for unity, the one-ness of mankind. But some people say it is also for Sarayana heaven, the place where the Gods reside."

"Interesting," Walt said.

"What happened to him? Your son?"

Walt swallowed. "He joined some kind of a cult, went to live at an ashram. One day the whole group took poison."

"I heard about that. In Gugarat, right?"

"Yes."

Simeone looked out the window.

"Have you been there?" Walt asked.

"Me? No. But I knew people who knew people who had, or said they knew people who had."

"The leader told them the end of the world was coming, and they would all help each other get to heaven by means of some kind of 'cumulative psychic release.' Isn't that a crock?"

"Who knows?" Simone said. "Maybe not. I haven't died yet, so I don't know what comes next, but it seems to me that something does. It must."

"They lay outside for several months before anybody found them. There was nothing left but bones. I don't even know if these are his bones, really."

"It doesn't matter. What matters is that you are with him in spirit."

"The leader left a note. He said the bodies would be in a pattern that would tell the rest of us how to achieve nirvana."

"Maybe it does."

"Sounds like a bunch of hooey to me."

"Have you seen the pattern?"

"There was no pattern. If there ever was, the jackals and hyenas and birds and things messed it up. And anyway, the authorities took up all the bones. If anyone saw, it would only have been them."

"You're still thinking on the physical plane."

"Say what?"

"Why do you think the pattern is visible?"

"What else could it mean?"

The fingers of Simeone's fight hand were interlaced with Walt's left. She patted his arm gently and smiled at him. "Why Katmandu?"

"He always wanted to go to Katmandu. He also wanted to take a road trip with his old man, you know, but I was always too busy working to take him." Walt's eyes began to tear.

"So here you are," she said, "you are doing it. How does it feel to be on the right path?"

* * *

The bus ground up a long grade for more than an hour, unbroken, before slowing to stop in what seemed like an endless line of traffic. The what-should-have-been-a-five-hour trip had stretched beyond ten, and now the sun was dipping behind the mountains in the west. Every few minutes the bus inched forward, then stopped, and the driver killed the engine and set his brakes. Walt had done the same many times passing an accident, a landslide, a road repair. But never in all his life had he been stopped by nervous soldiers with guns. Eventually they made the checkpoint. A half-dozen soldiers boarded the bus, behind them two men in civilian clothes, big men, with hard faces. Here it comes, Walt thought. They seemed to have something specific in mind, one of the civilians held a paper, presumably a list of names. They came past Walt to the man behind him and said something in Nepali. The man stood up. Behind the two plainclothesmen was a tall soldier with a Swedish K. The muzzle was uncomfortably close to Walt's ear. One slip...but what was it Simeone said? "When it's your time, it's time. You can't fight fate." The plain-clothesmen elbowed their way past the soldier. They had the passenger in tow, his hands bound behind his back with bailing wire twisted tight. Walt stared after them, watched them lead the man off the bus and into a make-shift barbed-wire enclosure.

Walt felt a tap on his shoulder. The soldier nudged him with the Swedish K. Don't go there, Walt thought, looking the man in the eyes and willing him to back off. The man looked down at the briefcase between Walt's legs. The brass lock looked very bright. "Open it," the soldier said.

"No," Walt replied.

The soldier prodded Walt in the chest with his gun, said "Open it" again.

"I am a citizen of the United States," Walt replied. "And you can't search my bags." Walt was bluffing. He was pretty sure the soldier could do anything he wanted, would do anything he wanted, and there was nothing Walt could do to stop him.

Passengers in the front turned their heads to look. Simeone hissed in his ear, "Are you crazy?" The other soldiers looked up attentively. Two of them walked down the aisle towards Walt. The soldier with the K knelt, letting his left hand fall from the gun to the lock on the briefcase. He fingered it lightly, still eyeing Walt, his right finger on the trigger.

"I'll open it if you want," Walt said at last. "I've got nothing to hide. But before I do, I want to know your name, and the name of your commanding officer." He slipped his hand inside his coat pocket and produced a pen and paper.

The soldier dropped the lock and reached his free hand up to Walt's neck. When Walt opened his jacket, Robbie's charms, Ganesh and Kali, fell exposed. The soldier fingered them delicately. At that moment, one of the plainclothesmen appeared at the door and barked an order in Nepali. There was no mistaking the tone, even Walt understood. *Let's go.* The soldier locked eyes with Walt, the corners of his lips turning up in what could have been a smile, but might have been a sneer, *I'll be seeing you.*

After they were gone, Walt realized that he was crushing Simeone's hand.

"That was wild," she said.

* * *

Once the bus started again, they quickly topped the ridge, and Walt could see Katmandu laid out beneath them in the gloom. It looked like something out of a bad science fiction movie. As far as Walt could see, the valley was filled with homes and factories and God-knows-what-all, a patchwork of buildings thrown together without plan and held together with sheer desperation; the whole scene obscured in a dense haze of blue-brown toxic smog. Half the buildings were unfinished, and Walt couldn't tell if there were going up or coming down. Empty lots were filled with piles of rubble, and everywhere people slung baskets from their heads, or pushed or pulled carts, or drove every conceivable manner of conveyance from donkeys and yaks and bicycle rickshaws to things that looked like garden tractors chopped in half and hitched to home-made wagons. They carried bricks or wood or sand or rebar. And when they crossed bridges Walt looked down into lifeless streams of industrial runoff and saw children playing in shallow, oil-slicked pools, women washing clothes, and people bathing, or gathering water in jars and pitchers and bottles.

And as the bus wound slowly down the hill, bound in traffic, pausing often to let local passengers off, it occurred to Walt that the soldier might make a report. The plainclothesmen might come after him. Walt wondered what was the worst that could happen? Could he be jailed for illegally transporting human remains across an international border? Walt had landed in jail once when he was a teenager, though he doubted that the lockup in Katmandu was anything like the one in Las Vegas.

As they drove, night fell, and fires sprang up all across the valley; inside homes, on rooftops, in the streets. And crowds materialized around the fires. The scene was bizarre. It reminded Walt of a tent revival his parents made him attend when he was twelve. A traveling evangelist expounded on the Biblical Gehenna, the Valley of Fires outside Jerusalem. Yes, Walt thought, I have seen the end of the world. When it all falls apart, America will look just like this. But strangely, Walt wasn't afraid. If it ends, it ends, so what? None of us live forever. When it's time, it's time. But though Walt was not afraid of death, he still chose to live. But what did that mean about Robbie?

Simeone had dug out her Lonely Planet guide.

"How old is this place?" Walt asked.

"About 2000 years," she replied.

"These buildings look like they were built to last 500 years," Walt said. "And they've been standing for 499."

* * *

The bus route ended in front of a storefront tourist agency on a crooked little street in Thamel District. Outside the bus, Simeone shouldered her backpack and shook Walt's hand. "What's next for you?" she asked.

"Find a room. Figure out what to do with Robbie. I've got to do something with his bones."

"And then?"

"Who knows? Would you like to...?"

"No," Simeone said, laughing. She leaned over and kissed Walt the French way, lightly on both cheeks. "I am meeting friends."

"Okay," Walt said. And he watched her walk away, astonished at how quickly she vanished into the crowd. It was like she had never been.

He sighed. For some reason, it did not bother him to be alone. What was she had asked, "How does it feel to be on the path?" He wasn't sure, but it wasn't uncomfortable. What it was he couldn't say. But he was certain the answer would come.

Walt turned and looked in the window. The agency was still open, a man inside gestured for Walt to come in. On the window were posters advertising tours of Katmandu, with photos of some of the sites: the Royal Palace, Dabar Square, Pashupati, the Swayambhunath Stupa, the Clock Tower. Walt's eyes lit upon a peculiar structure. It looked like a melting scoop of vanilla ice cream with a gold toothpick stuck on top. But what caught Walt's eye was the painting on the side, The Merciful Eyes of Vimochana. By now the tourist agent had come outside. "Can I help you?" He asked. "Hotel? Tour?"

"This place," Walt said, tapping on the glass. "What is it?"

"The Temple of the Monkey God," the agent replied. "I can book a tour for tomorrow morning. There is a ceremony going on. Very lucky for you that you come now, it only happens once a year."

"The Monkey God, huh?" Walt said. "Well that's just perfect."

Bread

I sat down on the porch with a cup of coffee and scratched Slacker behind the ears, and he smiled a mellow lab-dog smile. It's just for a little while, my friend Otto said, a week or two, until they can figure something out better than jail. "For Christ's sake," he said, "he's only a kid." A kid who starts fires.

A half-hour later, Otto pulled up in a blue Ford Explorer and got out, looking rumpled as ever, and the kid got out the passenger side, but I couldn't see him. I've known Otto forever, it seems—we went to high school together—and he sweet-talked me into this foster care thing a couple of years ago. "Look," he said, "it's just in case." I took that to mean never, hoped it meant never, and only filled out the paperwork to get Otto off my back. But never is a long, long time, they say, and two years later, here it is. I'm gonna be daddy again, if only for a couple of weeks.

Otto said something to the kid and hefted a brown paper grocery bag from the back seat. He was through the fence and halfway up the yard before the kid came around the front of the car. Jesus, I thought, how old is he? Otto said he was ten, but he's awfully short for his age.

Otto works for Child Protective Services and looks like it. Wrinkles fan out from the corners of his eyes, furrows crease his forehead, and his hair is thinner and grayer every time I see him. He still wears it pulled back in a ponytail (a holdover from his hippie days), and I imagine it's an act of defiance against the suit and tie the job requires. He's got a short, trim beard that's gone gray, too, and his head droops forward over his chest like a sunflower in September. He's skinny—he was always skinny—but while the years padded my belly, I think Otto's job gnawed him from the inside.

The kid stopped outside the gate like he'd never seen a picket fence before, like it was a prison enclosure and he was already planning his escape. He looked up and down the street. Nothing there but neat houses like mine, with big shade trees and decorative fences, trellises and flower gardens, birdbaths and lawn statuary. It was a hot afternoon. The finches warbled their short, pretty, irregular songs. Down the street someone started up a lawnmower. A crop-duster droned lazily overhead, slowly spiraling down towards the airport, or a field.

I know all my neighbors. Most of them are older, like me, our children grown and gone, except on holidays—when they come back to visit. They drive over the mountains from Seattle or Portland, or up from LA and San Francisco, in from Spokane or Billings or Boise, wherever they've gone to make their mark on the world. They sip wine coolers on the porch and reminisce, grandchildren toddling about the yard and gibbering, pointing out birds and squirrels.

From the moment the kid walked through the fence he looked down, not up. He wore faded blue jeans that were too long for his short legs and piled up on top of his sneakers, a blue and white baseball shirt, untucked, with the number 17 on the front. He wore a Mariner's baseball cap pulled down low over his eyes. The cap was old and the bill was bent. Red and black paint stains discolored it. His hair, scraggly and blond, stuck out from under it like thatch. It was the same color as the wheat fields out on the edge of town. On his back he carried a black nylon pack that was not very big. He had a little kid's baseball glove shoved in a net pocket on the side. A tattered blue *Sesame Street* 'Grover' poked his head from under the flap.

"This is all we could get for him on short notice," Otto said, setting the bag down by the screen door. I glanced into it and saw an assortment of old clothes, neatly folded, thrift shop tags stapled to them. "He took his pack out before he...well, he takes his pack everywhere. Anyway, we lost everything else in the fire."

Slacker got up lazily and nuzzled Otto's leg before sniffing the bag with considerable interest. He walked to the top of the steps and slowly wagged his tail, watching the kid. The kid scraped his feet along the sidewalk, still looking down.

"Look," Otto said. "Don't worry about the boy. He won't cause any trouble. He's plenty scared, and we've got him in intensive therapy. I'll pick him up at eight and bring him home in the afternoon, so you don't have to fix him lunch. Anything he needs now, you buy and give me the receipts. If he stays into next month we'll give you 287 bucks, and you take his expenses out of that. But I'm sure we'll find something before then."

The kid stopped at the foot of the steps. Slacker wagged his tail and hobbled down the steps, one at a time. He's an old lab and he's got bad hips, so he doesn't hurry anywhere, but especially on steps. He circled the kid cautiously, sniffing at his heels. The kid stood stock-still. I saw a big purple knot on his cheekbone, under his left eye. There was a cut in the middle of it, the slash swelling open like two lips and making a bright red line down the middle of the bruise. A black stitch straddled it like a spider.

Otto leaned close to my ear and whispered, "Foster dad slugged him. You got rid of the matches, right, gasoline, lighter fluid, stuff like that?"

I nodded.

"Good," he said. "Willie, come on up here and meet John. John, Willie. Willie, John. Shake hands, sport."

The kid stumped up the steps and stopped just beyond arm's length.

"You're gonna like John," Otto said, crouching down and facing him. "I've known him since we were kids. Me and him used to play baseball together. John had a helluva fastball. He was a pretty good short stop, too. If you ask him, maybe he'll teach you a thing or two."

The kid said nothing, and when Otto reached out to jostle his cap he flinched.

"Come on, Willie," I said. "I'll show you to your room."

Otto said, "I gotta go. Peg's holding dinner for me. I'll see you in the morning. Be good, Willie. I'll pick you up at eight."

I picked up the bag of clothes and opened the screen door, holding it for Slacker and waiting for the kid. He didn't move, and finally I gestured with my head *inside*, but he took his time.

The TV was on in the living room. The Mariners were playing the Blue Jays, and the kid hesitated before following me down the hallway to the spare bedroom. "This is your room," I said. Realizing it was far from his room, I added, "At least, we'll try to make it your room." I set the bag down and laid his things out on the bed. Two pair of white cotton socks, two pair of jeans (one too large, the other too small), a couple of tee shirts, a pale blue and pink sweatshirt that was obviously meant for a girl, and one pair of red, jockey-style underwear. "Well, buddy," I said, "looks like we get to go shopping."

I looked around the room and realized how lifeless it looked since my daughter left home. Gina had plastered the walls with posters of Brad Pitt and Leonardo di Caprio, U2, Sting, the Clash, and Madonna. I built her a trophy case to hold the collections of My Little Unicorn's and Cabbage Patch Kids it took her twelve years to complete. I never liked them anyway, and as soon as she was gone I got rid of all that girl stuff and replaced it with sensible landscapes and portraits of wildflowers. A nautical clock on the dresser measured the days in slow, even-metered clicks. This room is dead as a Motel Six, I thought, and I couldn't remember the last time I was in here for any reason but to vacuum or dust.

"We'll fix this place up," I said. "What do you want on the..." but when I turned around, the kid was gone. I walked down the hall to the living room where he knelt on the floor in front of the TV. Slacker wagged his tail, then sat down next to him, then laid down, and finally rested his head on his paws. The boy reached out his hand and petted Slacker on the neck, then gently stroked his hair.

I walked past them into the kitchen and a minute later the boy appeared behind me at the door. "I'm baking bread," I said. "Smells good, doesn't it. You ever had fresh bread before?"

He shook his head—no.

I opened the oven and pulled out the loaves, set the pans on top of the stove and basted them with a little egg yoke before setting them back in the oven. "That'll make a nice crust. They'll be done soon."

The kid went back to the TV and in a few minutes I took the loaves out and set them on the counter. He reappeared at the door. "They have to cool before we can eat them," I said.

He looked at me, then turned around without speaking. I wondered when he last ate, and remembered how hungry little kids get. Gina used to come home from school starving. Arlene—my wife—would have fresh bread cooling on the sill, and she would slap a slab of butter between two slices, and Gina would grab it and run down the street to play with the Gilchrist kids. Slacker, just a puppy then, bounded along behind her.

I shook one of the loaves out of the pan and whacked off a thick, steaming slice. "You like butter or jelly?" I called.

The kid came to the door and shrugged his shoulders. I got grape jelly out of the fridge and spread it thick on his bread. He took it and went back to the TV. I followed him out of the kitchen and asked, "Who's winning?"

He didn't answer. He ate his bread carefully, holding it with both hands, not dropping a crumb. Slacker eyed him sadly and smacked his lips. The kid slipped him a piece of crust.

I watched the kid watching the game. It was no pitcher's duel. The Mariners were winning twelve to something and had the bases loaded, again. When he finished his bread the kid kept his hands folded almost in his lap, low and in front of him like a short stop, leaning forward whenever the pitcher went into his windup. When a player came to bat he clinched his fists, one on top of the other, as though he were at the plate. "Come on, buddy," I said. "We'd better get downtown before the stores close."

The kid got up quietly and I caught him looking at me for just an instant—but then he looked down again and followed me to the door. "You can leave your pack," I said, but he carried it anyway.

We drove downtown to Penney's. "Is there anything you want?" I asked. He shrugged. I bought him two pair of jeans and two pair of shorts, a half-dozen tee shirts, socks, underwear, a new pair of sneakers, a sweater, and a hooded sweatshirt. He was real good about trying things on. He marched dutifully into the dressing room and changed quickly. He turned around when I said, "Turn around," and he didn't complain about anything. Outside I wondered, A hundred and ninety bucks! How can anybody raise a family these days? And I remembered buying clothes for Gina, and how I used to work up a lather over the bills when she and Arlene went shopping. The kid never said a word.

"You want a coke?" I asked. It was late, but still hot outside. We were sweating like pigs in no time. "Let's get a coke," I said.

We got a coke at a Skroggin's Deli down the street. Skroggin used to be a psychiatrist in New York, but he moved to Walla Walla and opened a deli to get out of the rat race. I come in sometimes for a sandwich or a mocha. He makes a mean corn beef and cabbage on rye. We play chess sometimes. Sometimes we just talk.

Skroggin was behind the counter. He's a bit older than me, but in better shape; a tall guy, bald-headed, except for a ring of gray hair like a Roman laurel wreath. He's got pork chop side burns, too, so he looks a little weird and out-of-place, like he ought to be serving beer in some western saloon, not lattes and sandwiches in a little town out in the wheat fields. "Hey, John," he said. Then looking down, "Who's the kid?"

"This is Willie," I said, suddenly struggling to remember the kid's name. "I'm looking after him for a few days. Maybe a week or two. He needed a place to stay."

Willie and I walked around the block with our cokes and passed a sporting goods store. I caught the kid looking sideways in the window at the baseball gear. "You want a new glove?" I asked, but he didn't answer.

I'll wait, I thought, I'll wait until he asks. I'll make him talk. But he didn't. After a while we went in and I bought him an Alex Rodriguez poster for his room.

We stopped at the video store and rented *Field of Dreams* on our way home and watched it after dinner. When I sent him to bed, he went without arguing. I gave him time to change before I came in to check on him. He was curled up under the covers, Grover tight in his arms. He used his backpack for a pillow. I reached out and stroked his hair, brushing it out of his eyes, and remembered when Gina was little.

I phoned Otto. "Look" I said, "don't I get some kind of instructions, history, anything? You gotta give me something to go on here."

Otto cleared his throat and explained that the kid was in the juvenile system, and when they have a criminal history the files get really complicated and he could only tell me a little bit. They thought the kid was about ten. They thought that because six years ago they found him abandoned in a bus station and the doctor who examined him said he was around four. But the kid was undersized from malnutrition, and wouldn't say anything, so they couldn't say for sure. Nobody knew why he started setting fires. At first they were little fires, then they got bigger. The most recent fire burned his foster home to the ground (that was confidential information, Otto said, because of the criminal proceedings). His foster father belted him hard enough that they sent the kid to the hospital for x-rays and stitches. But except for the cuts and bruises, and being undersized from childhood malnutrition, he was in pretty good shape. CPS brought him down from Spokane to relocate him—they thought a change in scenery might be good for the kid. He loved baseball, which was normal. He'd sometimes rock for hours in a corner, which was abnormal. He also wouldn't unpack his bag, and he wouldn't change clothes, or bathe with anybody in the room. In fact, Otto said, if I ever saw the kid naked, he would run away.

I lay awake that night wondering, what could do this to a child? And who? And why?

Slacker got up, walked to the door, and whined. I listened but my hearing's not so good, and I couldn't make out anything but the clock ticking. I got up, tiptoed to the door, and peeked around the corner. I heard a crash in the living room, and the kid raced down the hall into his room. I expected to see flames flickering in the dark, but there were none.

After a minute I turned on the light and went to investigate. Arlene's picture lay on the floor, the glass broken. I put it back on the mantel and checked on the kid.

He was curled up under the sheets like nothing had happened. He was in exactly the same position as when I first checked on him. "Listen," I said, "if you can't sleep, I understand, it being a strange house and all. But if you have to get up and move around, be careful, okay? That picture —that's my wife. She's dead now, and she didn't like having her picture taken, so I don't have many of her. I know you didn't mean to break it, but just be careful, that's all."

* * *

Otto showed up the next morning at eight on the button. I poured him a cup of coffee and gave him the receipts for the clothes. "I know," he said before I could grouse him. "We didn't have much time, and the kid burned everything. They got him that junk in Spokane before they brought him to me."

"He's slow this morning," I said. "I don't think he slept well last night."

"He'll get used to it. Come on, sport!" he shouted. "Time's a-wasting."

The kid came out of his room in the same clothes he wore yesterday. Slacker whined and pawed at the door when they drove off.

The kid's new clothes were right where I laid them out, folded neatly on his bed.

Later on Otto called. "I've only got a minute" he said. "Willie's eating a burger. About this sleep thing, maybe you can take him out for some exercise. Tire him out. That'll help. We're gonna be a little later than usual today. Judge wants to see to him in person."

When he hung up I said to Slacker, "Well, what do you want to bake today?"

* * *

Slacker perked up when he heard Otto drive up and the car doors slam. Otto walked Willie to the steps and left him there. The kid plopped down in front of the TV—it was off—and waited. "No game today," I said,

59

bringing him a slice of buttermilk bread. "It's a travel day. They play in New York tomorrow. Come on, we're going for a ride."

We drove to the park and when we got there I pulled a new glove out of the trunk and tossed it to the kid. He looked at the glove, holding it like it was porcelain. He pressed it to his face and smelled the leather.

"Go on," I said.

The kid ran a short distance from the car and turned around. He leaned forward and punched his fist into the webbing. I hit him a soft line drive, which he caught and threw back, the ball landing on the ground and rolling to my feet. I hit him a pop-up, which he caught, and another, which he lost in the sun and took off the heel of his glove. He moved where he wouldn't stare right up into it and I hit him a grounder, which he fielded flawlessly and ran back in.

"You do it," the kid said, holding the glove out to me.

I looked at the kid, he looked at me. "Okay," I said. I took the glove from him and held it in my hand. It felt heavy and stiff. I slapped the leather against my hand. It was a good glove. I would have killed for a glove like this when I was a kid. Give me six months and I'd have it soft as a dish-cloth. Otto said I was a great short stop, and he was right. I had wheels, a cannon for an arm, and a glove I called "Death Valley." I could hit too, but for average, not power. I loved baseball. I handed the kid back the glove. "I can't," I said.

The kid looked down at his feet. He mumbled, "Otto said you could teach me."

"I can teach," I said, "but I'm too old to play."

The kid looked across the park to a dirt diamond where a group of screaming boys played an impromptu game. "Go on" I told him. "It's all right."

"Let's me and you play," he said.

I hit and he caught until it was so dark I was afraid we'd lose the ball. "Let's go home," I said, "I'm hungry." After dinner the kid fell asleep on the couch while I was washing the dishes. I carried him to bed and tucked him in. I remembered Otto's warning, so I left him in his clothes. I laid Grover on his pillow where he would find him if he woke up.

My back ached from swinging the bat—it had been years since I played—so I took a pill for the pain, and if the kid got up during the night, I didn't hear him.

* * *

The next afternoon I baked croissants. Otto dropped Willie off early and he walked into the kitchen before I was done. "These are tricky," I said. "You have to roll them out so many times to get them flaky. You want to help?" I pulled up a chair so he could reach the counter and handed the kid a knife. He cut the dough into squares rolled them into crescents, then we popped them in the oven and, when they were done, ate them hot.

"You eat a lot of bread," he said.

"I love bread," I replied. "My wife..."

The kid looked up at me expectantly. The swelling under his eye was going down, but the bruise had spread from the tip of his lip all the way to his ear. The stitches will come out tomorrow, I thought, or the next day. He still wouldn't wear the clothes I bought him, and he took his backpack every morning when he left with Otto, Grover peeking out from under the flap.

"What happened to her?" he asked.

"She died."

"How?"

"She died in a car accident."

In the middle of the night I heard Slacker's tags jingle and I woke up. I crept to the door and looked down the hall. I caught a glimmer of light in the kitchen, a reflection off the wall, and I knew the kid was there. I listened for a while, sitting in the dark on the hardwood floor. I heard the kid pad down the hall almost to my door and stop—Slacker walked out and I heard the kid say, "Shhhhh." After a while he went back, to his room I suppose, and I fell asleep on the floor.

I felt like shit in the morning. Otto came. I asked the kid if he wanted to leave his backpack but he didn't. He did wear his new clothes, though, and that was something. I went into his room when he was gone and looked around. My bat stood in a corner, propped up against the wall. His new glove, and my old one, lay on the floor beside it. He had nested a ball in the webbing of his glove to break it in, just like I showed him. I gathered his dirty clothes in my arms and carried them downstairs to the laundry. I put his things in the washer, one by one, feeling them with my hands, reading the tags, checking the pockets. His old clothes—the one's he wore the day he arrived—had other people's names in them. He's a boy with no tangible past, I thought, no possessions, no identity, no roots. It's great if you're a Buddhist monk, but it's a lot to ask of a child.

In the afternoon I baked orange rosettes—one of my favorites—and they came out bang perfect. I had them cooling on the sill when the kid came in, but he walked into his room without saying a word and slammed the door.

I offered Otto coffee but he shook his head and patted Slacker absent-mindedly. "We took the stitches out," he said. "The kid put up a helluva fight. He hates doctors. It's the exams, you know."

I nodded.

"He gets like this, sometimes," Otto said. "You have to work around it, you know what I mean?"

I sent Otto home with a rosette for dinner.

The kid sat on his bed with his knees tucked up under his chin gazing out the window. "How 'bout we play some catch?" I said, but he didn't answer. "Maybe we could walk in the park—Slacker could use the exercise."

More silence.

"The game's on in a little while. Moyer's pitching."

The kid started rocking, slowly at first, then faster. Slacker whined and pawed at the bed, then jumped up and tried to lick the kid's face. The kid pushed him away and kept on rocking. Slacker tried to follow him, then pawed at the kids arm. Eventually he gave up and lay down at the foot of the bed to watch.

Where does he go? I wondered. What is it like in his quiet world?

* * *

I woke up in the middle of the night and something told me I should check on the kid. He was gone. The front door was chained and the back slider was locked, so I knew he was in the house someplace. I stopped at the top of the basement stairs and listened. There was a light on in the laundry room below. I smelled smoke.

The kid sat cross-legged on the floor with my photo album open on his lap. I hobbled down the stairs and sat next to him. He pointed at a picture of a little girl and asked, "Who's that?"

"That's my daughter, Gina," I said. I took that picture at the San Diego Zoo when she was twelve. And that's my wife. We used to travel a lot."

The kid lingered over the book, turning the pages slowly.

I looked at him and he looked at the book and it occurred to me he didn't know what a zoo was. "Do you know what a zoo is?" I asked.

He shook his head.

"It's where you go see animals. You know, like lions, and monkeys, and tigers, and elephants. You've seen animals on TV, right?"

He nodded.

"Do you have a favorite animal?"

He shook his head.

"Well, maybe we'll go, sometime. We'll drive over to Seattle and go to the zoo. They've got a nice zoo there. Would you like that? We could go to the zoo, and then we could get something to eat, and I could take you to Safeco Field and we could watch the Mariners play for real. We could sit in the outfield when they take batting practice, and you could put on your glove, and maybe catch a ball. Would you like that? You could catch a ball a real ballplayer hit. That would be something, wouldn't it? Would you like that?"

The kid shrugged his shoulders and I reached out to touch his arm but he pulled away. "Come on," I said, "I know you'd like it. We'll go to the zoo, but not tonight. Maybe next weekend. You go on to bed, now. I'll see you in the morning." The kid closed the book and trudged up the steps.

I looked at the book. The next picture was me and Arlene and Gina at Disneyland. I thumbed the pages: Gina's high school graduation, Gina and her roommate at college, Arlene and I in Hawaii for our anniversary. The last picture was Arlene and Gina baking in the kitchen, a picture I took on a whim trying out a new camera. The camera was a birthday present from Gina. Arlene is baking a big, round, dark-rye, peasant loaf, made with molasses. It was my favorite. She has flour smudged on her cheek and her hair has come loose. She is laughing, a wooden spoon in her hand. She's trying to keep me from taking her picture. "You wouldn't want to remember me like this," she said. It was the last picture in the book. I could smell burnt plastic in the air. I flipped through the remaining sleeves until I found the one the kid had burned. At least it was empty.

* * *

In the morning, after Otto drove the kid to therapy, I took his room apart piece by piece. I went through his clothes. I took the drawers out of the dresser, the sheets off the bed. I turned the mattress and box springs. I looked in the hollow tubes of the bed frame and took the poster of A-Rod off the wall. They had to be somewhere. I called Otto. He was in a meeting. I left a message. He didn't return my call.

I baked peasant bread. It was dark and sweet. I rolled it in oatmeal before I let it rise, so there were little crisp flakes in the crust when it was done. When the kid came home we ate some, then drove to the park. I hit him ground ball after ground ball and he fielded like a pro. And when he brought the ball in to me and wanted to bat. I took the glove and walked out to the outfield. Ball after ball sailed by wide right, left, under my glove, between my legs, over my head. "You suck," the kid said. "Otto said you could play."

"I used to."

"You're a liar," he said. "You're all liars." He turned and ran down to the field where the little leaguers played. He leaned against the backstop there and watched them play.

The kid was quiet during dinner. Later on, when he went off to take a bath, I slipped into his bedroom and searched his backpack. I went through the pockets and emptied the contents onto the bed. Grape flavored bubble gum, pennies, his sweatshirt, his new glove, and Grover. I held Grover up and asked, "Where do you come from? Why has he held on to you all these years?" Little balls of blue fur rubbed off Grover's skin. A few tired stitches held his right eye in place. His stuffing separated with age.

I tried to imagine Grover new, purchased hastily in a dime store someplace, downtown Seattle maybe, tucked under the kid's arm in a bus depot. The mother whispers a promise she knows she won't keep, then walks away, boards a bus for parts unknown. The child sits in the lobby with a backpack and a toy. He thinks, How will she recognize me when she comes?

I think, You're lumpy, losing your fur, you got too many loose stitches, you're old like me. You've outlived your time. You're coming apart at the seams. I squeezed Grover and felt something that wasn't cotton. I slipped my fingers inside a torn seam and pulled out a box of matches.

The kid was drying off in the bathroom. When I burst in he froze, clutching the towel to his body.

"Where did you get these?" I asked, holding the matches up for him to see.

"Get out!" he shouted. "Out! Out! Out!" He stood with his hands clinched in little fists under his chin, the towel in front of him. He was dripping wet.

"You want to burn my house down?" I said. "You want to burn my stuff? Go ahead, I'll help." I struck a match and threw it on the floor.

The kid looked down at the sputtering match.

"What's the matter? Not good enough?" I struck another match. "How 'bout on the carpet?" and I tossed one into the hall. The nylon melted and a small flame sprang to life, then died, leaving behind a whiff of acid-smelling smoke.

"What, try again?" I asked, throwing another match, and another one, and another.

The kid didn't move.

"How 'bout your stuff?" I said. "Mine doesn't burn so good. Maybe we should burn your stuff for a change, and see how you like it." I went back to the kid's room and came out with Grover. How 'bout old Grover?" I said. "Maybe he'd like a hotfoot?" I struck a match and held it to Grover's foot. A little flame sprang up and sent a strand of smoke spiraling towards the vent. The kid lunged at me, tore Grover from my hands, then slipped and fell.

I fell too, hard, and when I landed I caught the door jam with my elbow and my arm went numb. I lay on the floor and rubbed it, and then I looked at the kid.

He had lost the towel. His chest was laced with purple and white scars. He burst into tears.

"My God!" I said. "Who did that to you?"

The kid said nothing.

"You've got to tell sometime. You can't hold it in forever."

I sat on the floor, and the kid sat, looking at me. Then he reached out his hands and touched my shoes. He slipped off my shoes and socks, and stroked my flesh-toned plastic feet. He touched the hinges where they joined the titanium struts that serve me for legs.

"Arlene and Gina took me out for dinner," I said. "I don't remember the rest."

The kid sat very still.

"We were driving back from the tri-cities. The newspaper said a truck hit us. I woke up in the hospital three days later. They were gone."

The kid stood up and wrapped the towel around his waist. "She burned me. I don't remember, either, but that's what the doctor says." He picked up Grover and went to his room.

* * *

I woke him in the morning. We ate bacon and eggs, the kid dangling his spindly legs off the chair. They almost touched the floor. "I'd swear you've grown," I said.

Otto rang the doorbell at quarter to eight. "You're early," I said. "Willie's not ready."

Otto patted Slacker on the head.

"You want a cup of coffee?"

"We got a place for Willie," Otto said. "I came to take him."

"What do you mean...a place?"

"A place. You know, a home."

"Willie has a home," I said. I looked down the hall. The kid stood outside his bedroom, head down. He wore the ugly hat he wore the morning he first came over. He had his backpack on, the old glove stuffed in the side pocket, Grover peeking out from under the flap. He started down the hallway, but I put out my hand and stopped him.

"He's not leaving," I said.

"What are you, John—crazy?"

Slacker whined and pawed at my leg. "Willie's got a home," I said. "He's not going anywhere."

"John," Otto said, "let's not make this..."

"Let's not make it what, Otto? What? Another place he left behind? Another house that wasn't a home? Another bedroom that wasn't his? Another man that wasn't his father? Willie doesn't burn just because he was burned, Otto. He burns because he has no past. His whole life is a pile of ashes. And if he burns my house down too, so what? What have I lost? The kid stays, Otto. Do you understand me? He stays."

"We shouldn't have this conversation in front of Willie. Bring him down to my office and we'll talk."

"There's nothing to talk about."

"Be reasonable, John."

"Get out of my house."

Otto flushed red. Beads of sweat popped out on his forehead. "You don't understand, John, this is the State of Washington talking."

"I understand perfectly well, Otto. And so do you, so suck it up and go tell your boss Willie has a home."

"I'll call the police, John."

"Fine," I said. "I'll call my lawyer. Let's see who can get to the courthouse first."

Otto turned and walked out the door, slamming it behind him. A few seconds later he came back to the top of the steps. "Damn you, John!" he shouted. "I asked you for a favor! Do you have to turn stubborn on me?"

"Just go talk it over with your boss," I said.

Willie sat in the kitchen looking down at the floor.

"We can play ball," I said. "You wanna play ball?"

He shook his head.

"We can call Seattle and make hotel reservations. We can drive over and I'll take you to the zoo, and maybe we can catch a game at Safeco field. Would you like that?"

He nodded.

"Whatcha wanna do today? I asked. "You wanna bake some bread?"

"Okay."

"What kinda bread you wanna bake?"

"Crescents," he said. "Can we bake crescents?"

"Okay," I said. "Croissants it is." I got down the flour and salt, the yeast, sugar, eggs, milk, and butter. "These take time," I said. "It's a lot of work to make them right, but they're worth it."

Willie pulled a chair to the counter and stood on it while I measured out the ingredients and mixed them in a bowl. We let the batter rise, and then we worked it into dough. We rolled it out and cut it into squares, folding them carefully over four times. We chilled the squares in the fridge, and later on Willie rolled them into crescents and set them on the cookie sheet. We popped them in the oven. And then we sat on the floor, side by side, me and Willie, and watched them rise.

Split Decision

In the fourth round Tuffy Garza backed Trick Webster against the ropes and beat him low, to the belly and ribs, then making hay for the chin when Webster's elbows dropped. In the fifth Garza staggered Webster with a straight left that launched Webster's mouthpiece into the lap of a blonde hooker screaming from the second row. But that was six hours ago, and now Garza staggers in the street, drunk, looking for rocks to throw at his manager's window. Up and down the neighborhood, lights come on, doors and windows open. Garza heaves a rock and shouts, "Come out, you goddamn Jew!"

Meyers opens a window upstairs and leans out into the night. "Are you crazy?" he shouts. "Get in here before somebody calls the cops."

Garza hasn't showered since he stormed out of the coliseum. His face still glistens with oily sweat and Vaseline. His lips and cheeks are swollen, a grey-green mouse puffs under his right eye. He looks older than nineteen. Scars snake across his cheeks. His eyebrows are worn away.

Meyers is seventy, a two-fisted whiskey drinker who's smoked two packs of Camel no-filters a day for the past fifty-five years. But he is wiry with old muscles, too. He looks like he could still climb through the ropes and do some damage. He opens the front door wearing blue silk boxers and a white tee. "Whadda you want?" he asks.

Garza melts against the door jamb and hangs his head. "I want my fight."

Meyers' wife, Mary-Elizabeth, rustles down the hall. She's thrown on a thick white terrycloth bathrobe. She calls from the kitchen, "I'll make coffee."

Meyers steers the kid to a chair in the living room.

Garza drops in the chair and buries his face in his fists. A few minutes later Mary-Elizabeth sets a cup on a table by Garza's elbow.

Meyers clears his throat. "Your problem," he says, "is you never listen. First time I laid eyes on you, I knew you was trouble."

* * *

Meyer's gym was built from a converted warehouse on a cul-de-sac by the freight yard in the dock district north of the Navy Base in San Diego. Garza was just-turned fifteen when a cop named Murphy dragged him in. The gym was bright with hot stadium lights hanging from the rafters. There were three rings with fighters sparring in each. More lounged around a row of benches on the far wall lifting weights and spotting each other. Along the right-hand wall, still more fighters flitting among an assortment of heavy, medium, and speed bags, pounding out a staccato beat. To the left was a humid dressing room with a scale-encrusted tile shower, and next to it, in the furthest corner of the gym, reeking of tobacco, sweat, and whiskey, Meyers' office.

Murphy, the cop, was tall, ruddy, and broad-shouldered. He carried a middle-age paunch, and sported mass of scar tissue where his eyebrows ought to have been. "Got a scrapper for you," he said.

Meyers watched two novice heavyweights working on footwork in the ring: three steps forward, jab, three steps back, weave. "Another tough guy?" he asked, his back to them. His voice is a husky rasp.

"Seems to think so. Can't get enough at school. Counselor sent 'im to me."

Myers turned and sized up the kid. "What do I look like, a fuckin' psychiatrist? Is this a drop-in clinic? I ain't on the market for no flyweight spics."

"Fuck you," Garza said. He shook his arm free from Murphy's grasp.

Meyers gestured towards an equipment box by the ring. "Lace 'em up," he said.

Garza looked from Murphy to Meyers to the ring where the boxers, now panting and leaning on the ropes, also watched. He found a pair of gloves and slipped them on, then clapped his fists together.

Meyers cinched the laces and pulled a helmet over Garza's head, fastening it with a Velcro chinstrap. The helmet was too big—it wanted to tip over Garza's eyes. Meyers slapped Garza on the side of his head and shoved him towards the ring. "Get in," he said. The heavyweights climbed out. Garza climbed in. He bounced up and down on the taut canvas, shook his neck, worked his shoulders loose.

"So what's his problem?" Meyers asked.

"The usual," Murphy replied.

"He steal?"

"Not that I know of."

"Dope?"

"Don't think so."

"I got no use for dopers, kid!" Meyers shouted. "I catch you on dope and you're through." Turning to Murphy he said, "Family?"

"Father—who knows? Brother in prison. Got a sister in juvi for prostitution. Mother works the canneries."

"Piece of shit," Meyers said. He shook his head and frowned at Garza, "What are you lookin' at, Tuffy? Get busy."

Garza looked around. "What you want me to do?"

"Throw some punches, move. Show me how you're gonna take the title."

Garza circled the ring, tentatively, then picked up speed. He bobbed from side-to-side crouched, leaning slightly to his left, and flicked out a pair of quick left jabs. He ducked, circled right, and threw a left-right combo. He backed up, moving on his toes, then lunged forward with a left jab and followed it with an off balance right uppercut. As he threw the punch, his feet found a wet spot and he sprawled on his back on the canvas.

The gym erupted in laughter.

Garza leapt to his feet and pulled the helmet up from his eyes. A voice from the crowd counted, "six...seven...eight..."

"Impressive," Meyers said, motioning Garza out of the ring. "First fighter in the history of boxing TKO'd by his shadow."

Garza sat down on the equipment box and gnawed at the laces on his gloves.

Meyers waved him up. "Go beat the bag for a while, and try not to sprain your wrist." To the idle boxers Meyers shouted, "What're youz-all lookin' at? Get busy!" The training resumed: squeaking shoes, the smacks of glove on bag, a blur of conversation. The heavyweights lumbered up and into the ring.

Garza joined a knot of fighters at the medium bags at the far end of the gym. For the first minute he flailed away, peppering with an assortment of school-yard punches. Then his arms tired and he slowed down.

Murphy disappeared into the office. Meyers shouted at the heavyweights. They shifted to a new pattern: three steps right, jab, three steps left, parry. Meyers glanced at Garza once, twirling his right hand, motioning to keep busy.

After two minutes, Garza's arms ached so bad he could barely throw a punch. In five he could hardly hold his arms up. He wandered over to the water fountain, but with his gloves on, he couldn't turn the handle to get a drink. He sat down on a bench.

Meyers whistled and the fighters gathered around. He called Garza into the middle of the circle and told him, "Hit me." Garza looked left and right, then danced tentatively on his toes.

"This ain't no disco, Tuffy, I said hit me."

Garza threw an overhand right at Meyer's face. Meyers sideslipped and parried, spinning Garza to the left. Then he slipped in close and brought his right open palm into Garza's solar plexus. Garza's knees buckled, and he stumbled forward. Meyers, pivoting to let Garzy by, followed with an open hand to the back of Garza's head that drove him the floor. Garza bounced up. Meyers fired off a straight left, but Garza ducked, stepped inside, and threw an uppercut of his own. But instead of finding Meyers' chin he whiffed, and Meyers' open right hand slammed into Garza's ear and sent him reeling.

Garza hurled himself at Meyers, fists flying, but Meyers slip-stepped and snapped Garza's head back with an open palm to his chin. Garza tumbled backwards into Murphy's arms.

Murphy gripped Garza in a bear hug, lifting him kicking and squirming into the air. "What do you think?" he asked.

"He's skinny," Meyers growled, "and dumb. But he's got balls. Bring him back tomorrow. Get him some shorts and shoes, okay? Comprende, amigo? Shorts and shoes? Come back tomorrow and I'll work with you."

A squat, broad-shouldered, flat-nosed, coal-black teenager unlaced Garza's gloves. His hands were enormous. They could have gripped a shovelhead. Garza looked from the boy's face to the mass of knotty muscles fanning out from his neck and shoulders, down his pecs to his abs. Even his quads and calves bulged. The boxer jerked the gloves free from Garza's hands. "Name's Trick Webster," he said. His voice was deep as a cave.

Garza nodded.

"Ol' Meyers treat e'rybody like that the firs' day. You did good, though. You took it. After that, it g'is worse. Wait 'til you get in the ring wi'd me."

* * *

The next day Garza showed up in a pair of worn, high-top sneakers and faded, gray gym shorts emblazoned with the green-and-gold University of Oregon Fighting Ducks logo. The shorts were too big. Garza kept pulling them up. And the shoes were about worn out. But for three months Garza wore them every day, until one day he came to the locker room and found a pair of red Nike high-tops and black-and-white satin Everlast shorts in his bin.

In all that time, Meyer never said two words to Garza, though occasionally Garza caught Meyers watching from across the gym. He put Garza on a conditioning routine: lift weights every day for an hour, then run three miles. Afterwards, one of the more experienced boxers worked with Garza on footwork. Then he'd skip rope fifteen minutes, punch a speed bag for ten, and hit the shower. At the end of the day Garza hobbled out of the gym barely able to walk. But he kept coming back.

* * *

One day in November, Garza came to Meyers and asked when he would fight.

"What's your hurry?" Meyers replied.

"I didn't come here to punch bags."

Meyers led Garza to a heavy bag and patted it. "Show me what you got, Tuffy."

Garza fired off a high left jab and followed with a short, low right. He threw the left true and it smacked leather with a satisfying pop, but he threw the right like an uppercut, palm up, and when he hit the bag his wrist folded and Garza dropped to one knee. "Pundejo," he hissed.

"Get some ice on it," Meyers said, walking away. "And since you're not going to be lifting weights for a while, double your runs to six miles and tack on some wind sprints when you finish."

* * *

In February, when Garza turned sixteen, he asked again about fighting. The gym was closing, and most of the fighters had gone home. Meyer was in his office, a bottle of whiskey open on his desk. Across from him sat a mountain of black man, bearded, dressed in a camel-colored Kashmir wool suit with a black silk shirt. The man wore the shirt partly unbuttoned. Even so, his muscles threatened to rip it apart.

Garza knocked.

"Come in," Meyers said. "Oh, what do you want?"

Garza looked at the black man. "You a fighter?"

The man shrugged. He spoke in a slow drawl, but his voice was oddly high-pitched and raspy. "Some people say so."

"I'm a fighter, too," Garza said.

"Tha's nice." The man looked at Meyers.

"He wants to be a fighter," Meyers said.

"I am a fighter."

"Wha's yo' record?" the man asked.

"That's the problem." Garza fidgeted. "Mr. Meyers won't let me fight."

"Why not?"

"Says I'm not ready."

"Are you?"

"I think so."

"How come you want to fight? You mad or sumpin?"

"It's my destiny," Garza said. "First I'm gonna take the title off Ray Leonard. Then I'm gonna be the greatest fighter since Mantequilla Napoles. I'm gonna buy a house for me and another for mom."

"I hear that," the man said.

Garza asked, "Where you from?"

"South Car'lina."

"You should watch me sometime."

"I did."

"What you think?"

"I think you need time. Pu' some weight on."

"But I'm fast, right?"

"You okay."

"I'm fast like Sugar Ray."

"I seen Sugar Ray fight."

"You know him?"

"Uh hunh."

Garza smiled. "Tell him I'm gonna kick his ass."

"We call that sendin' a card. Who should I say called?"

"Francisco Garza."

"We call him Tuffy," Meyers said. "Go get your gloves, Tuffy, I got a fight for you."

"Right now?"

"Now."

"Who'm I gonna fight?"

"Him," Meyers said, pointing his glass at the black man.

The man pushed back his chair and stood. He looked more massive standing than he did sitting down. He held his hands at arm's length. "No thanks, Meyer. Tuffy too much for me." He left, brushing past Garza in the doorway. Garza could hear the fighter laughing as he crossed the floor; big, jerking belly laughs echoing in the gym.

"Sit down," Meyers said. He poured another drink.

Tuffy sat. "Look, Mr. Meyers, I can move, I can hit. I'm ready."

"Think so?"

"Yes, sir."

Meyer tossed his drink and grunted. "How's school?"

"Okay."

"Murphy says you been cuttin' class."

"Nah, man, I ain't been doing nothing."

"I ain't been do-in' nut-in'," Meyer said, rolling his head from side-to-side. "Don't fuck with me, Tuffy. Whadaya doing? Dealing? Boosting? A little shoplifting maybe?"

"No, man, nothin' like that."

"Don't bullshit me."

"I got a job, tha's all."

"You? A job? This I gotta hear. You gonna be the great American success story? Poor Mexican makes good? What kinna job you got, Tuffy? Washin' dishes?"

"Nah, man, I got a uncle drives a truck. Sometime he give me a little scratch to help load out, that's all."

"You skip school to load a truck?"

"Yeah."

"You dumb bastard."

"What do I need school for? I'm gonna be a fighter."

"All my fighters get diplomas, Tuffy. That's Meyers' Law. I don't push no dumb fighters. You quit school, you quit the gym. Go someplace else. Go see Faranelli, fight for the wops. What do you need money for, anyway?"

"I got a girlfriend."

"She pregnant?"

"No."

"Well thank God for that." Meyers said. He tossed his whiskey and poured another.

"I could make some money if I fought," Garza said, "I just need a few bucks to spend on my girl, you know. Show her I'm a regular guy, not some dreamer."

"But you are a dreamer."

"I can make it, Mr. Meyers. All you gotta do is say the word. I can go, I feel it. You seen me spar. Those chumps can't lay a hand on me."

"Those chumps can't hit their ass in the shower, but they don't lay a hand on you because they don't want to lay a hand on you. You're a kid, and even they know better. This girl, she got a name?"

"Theresa."

"Ta-reese-ah. How sweet. She a nice girl?"

"Yeah. You want to meet her?"

"What am I, your fuckin' father? I don't think so. She Catholic?"

"Yeah."

"A nice Cath-o-lic girl. You use a rubber?"

Garza blushed.

"Look, kid, I don't want to lose you to no fuckin' job. That's how this shit starts, see? First you fuck the girl, then she gets preggo, then you get a job and quit boxing. I been down that road before. So if you're thinking about fuckin' this fuckin' dame, then you better use a rubber, unnastand?"

"Yes, sir."

"It's not like I got no heart. I don't want you in no trouble, that's all. You got talent, Tuffy, anybody can see that. But you gotta be patient. You ain't ready."

Garza left the office, head down.

Meyer called him from the door. "I didn't get into this racket by bein' stupit, Tuffy. You're too skinny. You move okay, but you keep lookin' for the one-punch combo. I tell you you're not built for the knockout, but you don't listen. You can't take a punch, either. You get your weight up to one-forty, then I'll think about settin' you up. Until then, stay in school.'

Garza nodded.

"And another thing, starting tomorrow you stay late and clean up.

I'll give you what your fuckin' uncle was payin' you."

Garza's face lit up. "Really?"

"Really. Now beat it. Go find what's-her-name."

Garza stopped at the front door. "That fighter—"

"Yeah."

"He looked...I thought I mighta seen him before. Who was he?"

"Joe Frazier."

* * *

In June, Meyers showed up at Garza's apartment. Tuffy lived with his mom in a two-story, flat-roofed, concrete-block, Section 8 complex. It was not yet noon and 101° in the shade. Garza's mother called Tuffy to the door.

"You gonna ask me in?" Meyers asked.

Garza looked at his mother and she nodded.

The only light inside came from a TV. There was a Mexican League soccer match on. An older man in plaid shorts and a tee shirt drank Budweiser on the couch. There was a stack of empties on the floor. The man looked up but said nothing. Garza's mother was cooking, frying peppers on the stove. "How's things?" Meyers asked.

"Okay."

"Your sister, she's okay too?"

"She took off again."

"That's too bad," Meyers said. "If she turns up, tell her to come and see me. I'll find her an honest job."

"Que quieres?" Garza's mother asked.

"El quiere dar Sylvia un trabajo," Tuffy replied.

"Dígalo irse," she said.

"She says thanks."

Meyers nodded. He said, "I got tickets to see Hagler in Vegas. You wanna go?"

Garza's eyes lit up. He turned to his mother. "El quiere tomarme reunir Marvin Hagler."

"Bullshit," the man on the couch said.

Meyers looked at the man. "This doesn't concern you," he said.

The man stood up. He hadn't shaved; his hair hung in long, greasy locks; his eyes were bloodshot. He pointed a finger at Meyers.

Before he could speak Meyers said, "Siéntese antes yo atasco esa botella arriba su como."

The man sat down.

* * *

Meyers, Webster, and Garza left at noon the following day in Meyers' Lincoln. The fight was at Caesar's Palace and they had good seats. Not ringside, but close. Meyers seemed more interested in the prelims than the main event. The first two were yawners but the last was a war. An LA lightweight named Tony Bonelli TKO'd a Cuban named Ortega. Ortega's hands were light lightning, and he pressed the attack the first six rounds, but Bonelli fought him methodically, covering up and weathering the storms until the seventh, when Ortega tired. Once Bonelli smelled blood he exploded with a barrage of punches that left Ortega on the ropes and bleeding. The doctor stopped the fight when the cuts reopened in the eighth. Ortega's trainer jumped up and down in the ring—had to be restrained from going after the ref—and even a couple of fans got in the melee and were hauled off in handcuffs. It was quite a show. Hagler won his bout easily, decking an older fighter three times in the first before finishing him in the second.

After the fight Meyer drove Webster and Garza to the MGM Grand. "We're gonna meet some people," Meyers said, handing his keys to the valet outside. "Keep your mouths shut. You speak only if spoken to and keep your answers short—five words or less, Tuffy. I know what a motor-mouth you are. You can say, 'Yes sir,' 'No sir,' and 'Thank you.' Not one word else, got it?"

They ate in a private dining room. Don King sat at the head of the table, Hagler on his right, a pair of busty blondes in matching red-sequined dressed on either side of them. Garza was surprised to see the Cuban, Ortega, there, too. Webster and Garza were introduced in a blur of half-hearted hellos and how-are-yous, the only names catching Garza's ear being Luciano Faranelli and Tommy Nolasco. Garza had heard their names on TV, mostly described on the news as reputed mobsters. After dinner, Meyers gave Garza and Webster each room keys and a hundred bucks worth of slot tokens.

"Where are you going?" Garza asked.

"Poker game," Meyers replied.

Garza and Webster wandered the floor until Webster hit a slot for five thousand bucks and vanished.

Garza tried to sneak into a strip club down the street, but the bouncers threw him out. He was picking himself off the sidewalk when Faranelli appeared. "Hey, kid," he said, motioning to Garza. "Meyer's know you're out?"

Garza nodded and Faranelli smiled. Faranelli was well over six-foot, broad shouldered, dressed in a smart, gray suit and a bright blue silk shirt. He was smooth-faced, with a broad, easy-going grin that flashed a row of perfect white teeth. "Come with me," he said.

They walked into the club, Faranelli nodding to the tight-mouthed bouncers, Garza strutting. The stage was lit with blue light, the bar with red. The sound system blasted Tina Turner's "Private Dancer" at ear-splitting level. Faranelli took a table below the stage. Tommy Nolasco was there, and another young Latin Garza took for a fighter, and two half-naked young women; one white, one Latina. A small-breasted blonde wriggled naked on the stage practically in their faces. A barmaid brought them a round of margaritas and a within minutes they were joined by two more girls. One of them was a young mulatto wearing a black teddy over sheer panties and no bra. She leaned on Garza. Her breath was hot in his ear.

Nolasco introduced Garza to the other fighter, a smooth-faced kid from Mexico City named Gonzales. Nolasco seemed pretty high on Gonzales' chances. He kept his hand on Gonzales' forearm. He asked if Garza wanted to fight in LA. Garza nodded. After a while Faranelli came around the table and chased off the mulatto, swatting her on the ass as she stood up. He sat next to Garza. "How good is this kid, Webster?" he asked.

"He's good."

"Will he stay a welterweight or move up to junior middle?"

"He's beefing up."

"What's his best punch? How's his defense? He got any weaknesses?" Faranelli ordered another round of drinks, and then another. After a while, Garza got woozy. He felt remote and far away, as though he were standing in a little room inside his head, looking out through his eyes like windows. His lips were numb. Faranelli got up and the little mulatto came back. She gripped Garza by the arm, her left breast crushed against him. She was sweetly perfumed, a scent more intoxicating than the tequila. The evening blurred. They left in a limo, dropping Garza and the girl at the hotel. In the elevator she whispered in his ear that her clit was pierced. She licked her teeth and smiled. Then she took his hand and showed him. She was gone in the morning.

Meyers was in a chair when Garza woke up. "Get up," Meyers said.

Garza staggered to the bathroom and threw up. His head pounded. Room service brought coffee, aspirin, and a bowl of menudo. Meyers sat by the window smoking cigarettes, lighting one from the butt of the other. "Where were you last night?"

"I was out."

Garza sniffed. The perfume was still faint in the air. He looked at the bed—thoroughly trashed. "Was she worth it?"

Garza looked away.

"Ever been drunk before?"

"No."

"Don't get in the habit. It's tough to break."

Garza stirred his menudo with no enthusiasm.

"Where's Webster?" Meyers asked.

"I don't know. He hit a jackpot and disappeared"

Meyers shook his head. "I shoulda known better than to trust you two."

* * *

Meyers pulled up to in front of Garza's apartment and handed Garza two, crisp, one-hundred dollar bills. "You saw the fight, you had dinner, you came home. You didn't see anybody and didn't talk to anybody. Right?"

"Right," Garza said. He went to shut the door but Meyers pushed it back open and held Garza's eye. "Buy something nice for what's-her-name," he said.

* * *

Two weeks after the trip, Meyers was closing the gym when a girl appeared in the doorway. She was short and thin, pale-skinned, with flax-colored hair and dark brown eyes. She wore jeans with a white cotton

80

sleeveless blouse. "Mr. Meyers?" she asked.

Meyers sized her up. "Step into my office," he said. Once in, he gestured to a chair. "Sit down, Theresa."

"Francisco..."

"Tuffy."

"Is my boyfriend."

"And you came to me to make him quit boxing."

"How did you know?"

"I know everything."

"Then you know about..."

"Why should I?"

"Why should you what?"

"Make him quit."

"Because he's a good person."

"So, you make him quit."

"He won't listen to me."

"He won't listen to me, either."

"Then make him."

"How?"

"I'm sure you have your ways."

Meyers looked Theresa over. Her eyes were wide, her mouth small, her lips full, her complexion clear. For a girl of sixteen, she kept her cool. Meyers could see the lace of her bra through her blouse. A little gold crucifix glinted from a chain around her neck.

She leaned forward and looked Meyers in the eye. "What do you know about Francisco?"

"He's got good balance, quick feet, fast hands, good instincts. He still looks for the knockout, but he's starting to bulk up. His uppercut'll get the job done."

"I mean, outside of boxing."

"I know he's smart and a hard worker. Tough, but he seems to have his head on straight."

"Then what do you want to mess him up for?"

"He came to me."

"He was brought to you."

"Same difference."

"No it isn't. He trusts you."

"So?"

"You're using him."

"Of course I'm using him. I run a gym."

"I thought maybe you were trying to straighten him out."

Meyers opened his desk and pulled out a bottle and two glasses. He poured himself a shot and then held the bottle over the other glass. "Drink?" Theresa shook her head. He poured the glass full anyway. "I'm not in the business of shrinking heads."

"What happens if he fights?"

"Maybe he wins."

"And maybe he loses."

"It's the name of the game."

"I meant, what happens to him?"

"He gets his share."

"How 'bout to us."

"You get your share."

"And you get yours?"

"I always get mine."

"Win or lose?"

Meyers tossed his whiskey. "Either way."

Theresa's eyes moistened. "You don't know him like I do, Mr. Meyers. He's a good person. He's got potential. You know how hard it is to be good in the barrio?"

"What do you know about good people, Theresa?"

"I may be young, Mr. Meyers, but I gave Francisco my heart. And when a girl like me gives her heart, she gives it for keeps."

"Tuffy says you like him fighting."

"I like him in the gym. Before he came to you, he was in trouble all the time. Now he stays in school, does his work. I want him to grow up and be a normal life."

Meyers picked up Theresa's glass. "What'll you do if he chooses boxing?"

"I'll leave."

"Maybe I know Tuffy better than you think."

* * *

Halfway through his junior year Garza bounced into the Gym and announced that he and Theresa were engaged. It was December and it had been raining for a week. There were buckets catching drips all over the gym. It got so bad Meyers had hired another kid to help Garza clean up.

Meyers was crouched by the center ring watching two middle-weights spar.

"Okay," he said, holding out his hand and not looking up. "Gimme your keys."

"What?"

"Gimme your keys. You're getting' married, you're through."

"But I haven't started."

"You think what's-her-name's gonna put up with a fighter for an old man?"

"Theresa loves me."

"She might," Meyers said. "But she'll never be a boxer's wife."

"Whachu mean?"

"Say I get you a fight and you win. The next might be in Reno, and the one after that in Sacramento. Then you go out to Jersey for a weekend, and a month later you're in Portland, Mexico City, Montreal. You think all your fights are gonna be here, Mr. Home-Team? A fighter lives out of a suitcase. You think she's gonna put up with that?"

Garza shrugged. "I suppose."

"And then there's the whole celibacy thing."

"Celibacy?"

"Yeah, you know. No fucking, no blow jobs, no spanking the monkey, nothing."

"I thought that was just some Hollywood bullshit."

"You thought. Ask the guys. You think sweet little what's-her-name's gonna put up with sixty days of no sugar? I don't think so."

"Sixty days?"

"And then there's the girls hanging round the back door of the coliseum, the hotel lobby, the bars. There's a whole dumpsterful of trashy girls out there hoping to fuck a fighter. You think you can handle that, Tuffy?" He looked at Garza and frowned.

Garza looked away.

"And another thing. Look at them fighters."

Garza looked. "What?"

"Tell me what you see?"

"Blue trunks locks his front knee," Garza said, "and he fights flat-footed. When red throws a left, he can't back out."

"Where can he move?"

"Into the punch or down."

"And if he moves down?"

"He can't see."

"And what'll red do?"

"Bring a right to the ribs."

"And then?"

"When blue drops his hands, he'll come across with the left again."

"He should, but will he?"

Garza watched red. He was taller than blue, but not as well-built. He harassed blue with his reach, but never finished his combos. "No," Garza said.

"Why not?"

"He's got his toes straight ahead."

"Meaning?"

"He's afraid."

"Right," Meyers said. "He's waitin' for blue to rush him. He's scared of that big right hand."

"Blue's got a punch."

"He's got a freight train, but that don't mean you stand on the tracks until it hits you."

"No sir."

"So what would you do?"

"Side-to-side. Keep centered and when he moves in, spin away, parry the hands and counter."

"Hit and run?"

"Hit and hit, I never run."

Meyers shook his head. "You're good, Tuffy, but you got it all wrong. You see two fighters in the ring. I see meat on the hoof. A paycheck. And I'm not talking about the purse. That's chump-change. I look at those guys and I see Murphy, a rummy ex-knocker holding down a job as a beat cop. And a thousand other used-up coulda-beens. It's no life is no life for a married man, Tuffy. You gotta make a choice here, boy. You can't do both. When you graduate?"

"June a year."

"I got first-hand information you was on honor roll last spring."

"I did alright."

"You did more than alright, Tuffy, you did good. Take my advice. Go to college. Marry sweet little what's-her-name and give her a bunch of bambinos. Make something of yourself. Keep her as far away from this place as you can. Forget you ever came here. My Mary, she's never set foot in the gym. She's never been to a fight. You come in my house, you'd think I was some kinda goddam doctor or something. My place got class. That the kind of place you want live in?"

Garza nodded.

"Then take my advice. Go to college. Get outta town."

"Don't you think I can be a champion?

Meyers put his arm around Garza. "I ever tell you how I got into this racket?"

Garza shook his head.

"Come, have a sit in my office."

Meyers poured a whiskey. "My old man come from Russia, but he got in the German camps during the war. I don't know how, and he never talked about it. Maybe he was in the army. Anyway, when the allies liberate the camp he gets to America. I don't know how he done that, either, but he did. He gets into school but he don't like it so he drops out and takes a job as a stevedore. This was in New York. After a while, he meets my mom. She's Russian, too, a real beauty. Workin' in some bar. They shack up, and then my dad gets in some kind of scrape and gets in jail. So while my old man's doing time, he gets this cellmate who's tight with the mob, see? And this guy's got this fight racket going, mostly in Jersey, but some out west, too."

"What's his name?"

"Raffone. He's dead now. But here's my point. Raffone and my dad get tight in jail, only Raffone gets out first, so he promises to look out for pop's interests on the outside. This is what guys in prison do for each other, see? So Raffone pays my mom a visit, just to see if she needs anything. But right away there's trouble—he's goes nuts for my mom. Raffone takes care of her, alright. And when my dad gets out of prison and comes home, Raffone finds him a job at a gym. That way Raffone can keep his eye on him, if you know what I mean, avoid complications. My old man, he's not dumb, he knows what's going on. But being a pragmatist, he keeps his mouth shut. I mean, it ain't like he wasn't getting any on the side, too. So he works his way from janitor to trainer, and trainer to manager. When Rafonne died, it passes down to him. And when he died, it came to me. After a while, I come out west to take care of things for the boys. Are you getting' the picture here, Tuffy?"

"You tellin' me this business is dirty?"

"Is a cat's ass pussy? Listen to me, Tuffy, you ain't never gonna be champion. It ain't in the cards. You fight, you'll end up punchy like Murphy, or like that slab you watched Hagler tattoo in Vegas. You know how much he got for that beatin'? Ten grand. That what you want to do with your life?"

"You gotta do this for me, Mr. Meyers."

"You hear a word I said?"

"I spent two years training, you owe me."

"I owe you? This I don't believe. I take you in, buy you clothes, give you a job, and now I owe you? Suit yourself, Tuffy."

* * *

Two months later Garza weighed in at one forty-five and demanded that Meyers line him up with a fight. Meyers, who'd had a bout of phlebitis, was watching center ring from a lawn chair. "No can do, amigo," he said.

"How come?"

Meyers sighed. "You're too young, you gotta be eighteen to fight in this state."

"But I know guys younger than me who fight golden glove all the time."

"How sweet. My wife, Mary Elizabeth, could take half of them."

"Tha's bullshit."

"You seen her fight?"

"That's not what I mean. There's lots of guys fight in Golden Gloves who aren't eighteen."

"But they don't fight for money. You don't believe me, call the boxing commission. I can't fight you 'til you turn eighteen."

* * *

The following June, when Garza turned eighteen, Meyers lined up a Cherry Popper, an opener featuring two first-time fighters. It was a

Saturday night in downtown LA.

"Nervous kid?" Meyers asked.

Garza shook his head.

"At least you're up first."

Garza had been working hard since graduation, loading truck in the daytime and boxing in the evening. His weight shot up to 153, putting him in as a junior middleweight. He had bulked up, but there was more. There was an edge to his training that was missing before. He showed up early and stayed late. He rarely spoke and never complained. His footwork was fluid and his punches crisp with a finish that rocked even the heavy bags.

"Time," Meyers said. They walked out the tunnel and down the aisle to the ring. To his surprise, Meyers saw tears in Garza's eyes. "Whatsa-matta, kid?"

"Theresa broke up with me."

"Ah, jeez, kid, this is not the time for this shit." He stopped Garza and spun him around, took his shoulders and shook him hard. "You gotta stay focused."

Garza nodded.

"When you step out there, it's gonna sound like the whole goddam world is in the bleachers. Turn out the noise and look around. Move, get a feel for the canvas. This ring is just like the one in the gym—twenty-two foot square. Don't hurry. Don't try to do too much. You're scheduled for eight. If you get in a rush, you'll pick up all your old bad habits. Give it a few rounds to settle in."

Garza nodded.

"Then kill him."

The referee climbed into the ring and the crowd roared. Suddenly Garza remembered something he had read in school about lions. Lions roar into the ground to confuse their prey. The sound scatters, it seems to come from all around. Garza heard the roar and felt naked. He sensed malice in the crowd. His heart raced and his ears rang. Then the noise and lights faded, he thought he might pass out. Meyers pushed him to his feet and he met the referee in the center of the ring. Garza didn't hear a word of the instructions. He touched gloves with the other fighter.

The bell rang, they circled. Tuffy threw a punch, took a punch, and then the situation came into focus. Theresa was gone. A rage boiled up in Garza's chest. He threw a punch and missed, then another that glanced. He took a shot to the mouth and tasted blood. Then he broke like a wave on the other fighter. It was over in less than a minute.

Nine fights and eight months later, he was still undefeated.

Then came the fight with Webster.

* * *

Meyers settled into a plush red-velvet Ottoman across from Garza. "A big God-damned shame," he said.

Garza hands trembled, his mouth twisted. "I ain't even cut."

"You're worse than cut, kid, you're finished."

"I knocked him down in the eighth."

"You're dead, you just don't know it."

"One more round and I'd have KO'd him."

"Kaput."

"I'm nine and one."

"And Webster's twenty-three and three. Did you really think you had a chance?"

"I'm better."

"Since when did better have anything to do with it?"

"Who put in the fix?"

"Does it matter?"

"It does to me."

"And nobody but you."

Garza stood up. "I'll go to LA. I'll get another shot. You ain't heard the last of me."

"Go on, go to LA. Go see Tommy the No. He'll remember you. But I promise you this, you're never gonna get a shot at the title. That was decided a long time ago."

"When? How?"

"In Vegas. Over cards."

"Bullshit."

"We got millions of dollars invested in this gig, kid. You think we're gonna screw it up leaving decisions to a buncha dumb fighters? I told you a long time ago, but you wouldn't listen."

Garza sat down. "What do I do now?"

"The name Jimmy Wilde mean anything to you?"

Garza shook his head.

"How 'bout Freddy Welch? Sam McVey? Harry Greb? Johnny

Dundee?"

Garza stared.

"They was all great fighters once. But today," Meyers shrugged his shoulders, "who cares? If it was me, and I was nineteen, and had my whole life ahead of me, I'd get a part-time job and sign up for community college, figure out some other way to make a living."

Garza sighed and looked away. Then he got up and went to the door. Meyers followed him. "Want me to call a cab?"

"I'll walk."

"Don't think too hard, kid, or take too long."

Garza crossed the lawn, but Meyers called him from the porch. "How long since you saw old what's-her-name?"

Garza looked at him blankly, then said, "Theresa?"

"Yeah, her."

"Six months."

"I have it on good authority she gives her heart for keeps. If I was you, I'd look her up."

"How would you know?"

"I know everything, kid."

Garza paused, looked down the street and then back at Meyers. "You think she'd take me back?"

"You wanted to be a fighter, kid. Ask yourself what's worth fighting for. Tell her that. Tell her you thought it over and figured it out."

After Garza was gone, Meyers stood on the porch. Mary Elizabeth came out and hugged him from behind. "That was some line you fed him," she said.

Meyers shrugged.

"Do you think he'll call her?" she asked.

"I'd say the odds are even-money."

"You're a good man."

"It's a Mitzvah," Meyers said, "what you do to make up for what you did. May they shout it up in heaven, my old man used to say, but keep it under wraps on earth."

Dead Water

Rex was the senior crewman so he always drove. The new kid was riding in the back, resting his chin on the on the seat between us like an old dog I used to have. I was navigating and didn't know where the hell we were. It was five-thirty in the morning and foggy as all get-out. I could see about fifty foot in front of us. We might as well have been driving through a cotton bale. I had a map spread out on the dashboard in front of me.

"You're about as useless as tits on a boar hog," Rex said.

The kid laughed, and I shot him a sideways glance.

"If you'd slow down," I said, "I might could make out a sign somewhere."

"No matter, we'll get there."

"We could ask somebody," the kid said, but when Rex and I glared at him he shriveled it up into a question, "Couldn't we?"

"And what the fuck are we supposed to say?" I asked. "'Scuse me, sir, I know it's five o' clock in the morning, and I don't mean to wake you, but could you please tell me where I am?"

"I'm just trying to find the bridge," the kid said, "where's that confounded bridge?"

"What the fuck are you talking about?" Rex asked.

"Led Zeppelin."

Rex might be the only man in Louisiana who never heard of Led Zeppelin. He plays accordion in a zydeco band called the Mud Mountain Mamas and he don't know shit—or care—about life outside of Iberville Parish. If you look up "redneck" in the dictionary, it's got his picture there. But when he's in uniform, you can't tell how bad off he is.

"You sure he's twenty-one?" Rex asked.

It was the kid's first day on the job and he didn't look a day over sixteen. He wasn't tall and he wasn't muscular, maybe five-eight and one-seventy, tops. He had a wispy little blonde moustache and a gold ring in his ear. I wouldn't have figured him to make it through basic training, but he had. With honors, supposedly. Head of his class.

"Couldn't nobody hardly blame us for being lost in this fog, could they?" the kid said.

"Put your seatbelt on," I said. "It's regulation."

The kid sat back in his seat, but didn't put his belt on. He had this nervous, high strung look rookies get on their first call. We generally let them mind the truck for about a month before we get them involved; bore them to death until they let their guard down. The last thing I need is a rookie trying to think.

Rex steered with his elbows while he poured himself a cup of coffee.

"You want a doughnut?" I asked.

Rex reached in the bag and pulled out a cream-filled. "How would it look?" he said, "us pulling up and asking directions? I mean really, what would people say? Goddamn fire department out lost, driving around in the woods. Waste of good taxpayers' money."

"But aren't we supposed to be looking for somebody?" the kid asked.

"Some *body*," I said. "They already dead, so it ain't no hurry. 'Sides, it's still too dark to get the boat out."

Rex stuffed the doughnut in his mouth and swung the Blazer off on a side road that gaped suddenly out of the fog. "Shit," he said, taking the doughnut out of his mouth, "I dropped a wad of cream in my lap."

"Looks like you came in your pants," I said.

"Fuck you."

The kid laughed and leaned over the seat between us again.

"I knew we'd find it," Rex said. "You got a napkin?"

I looked in the bag, then in the glove box. I shook my head.

"Just like a gook to skimp on a damn napkin." Rex untucked his shirt and scraped up the filling, then licked his fingers. "Fuckers sure can cook, though."

"Did you say gook?" the kid asked.

"Put your seatbelt on," I said.

"I didn't think we were supposed to slur people."

"Shut up, kid."

* * *

The call came in about 2:30. Cops in Donaldsonville found a car abandoned on the bridge. The keys were in the ignition and it wasn't stalled. That meant one thing.

"How'd they know it was a woman?" the kid asked.

"Maybe she left a purse," Rex said. "I dunno. It seems like it's almost always women what jump."

The kid looked thoughtful. "Seventy-five percent of jumpers are women," he said. Then looking around apologetically he added, "That's what they taught us in school, anyhow."

"I wonder if it's so," I said to nobody in particular.

Rex nodded and slurped his coffee, then fiddled with the radio for a minute and made it screech. He's been with the department thirty-nine years and he's about seen it all. "Man'll face right up to things," he said, "but a woman..." He hit the brakes sharply and the truck lurched to one side and skidded to a stop. "Jesus!" he said. He spilled coffee all over the dash.

I turned my head in time to see a buck bounding across the ditch and out of sight. "Did you see the rack on that bastard? He musta been a ten point, at least."

"Eight," the kid said.

"Whatever." Rex grabbed the map and used it to mop the dash. "You won't see him come hunting season."

Rex handed me what was left of the map. "Great," I said. It was soaked in coffee and falling apart in my hand. "Now what?"

"Map'll only getcha where you're goin' if you know where you are." He let off the brakes and the truck eased forward, and for just a moment the fog lightened up. "And I know where we are. So, a man'll face up to things—just blow his head off with a shotgun. But a woman hasn't got the nerve. She's always thinking 'what if...' So she'll jump, you see, so there's a chance she might make it. Women like to be talked out of things, but a man'd just as soon shoot hisself."

"Women don't like to be messed up," the kid said.

"What are you talking about?" I asked. "I know lots of messed-up women."

"Their corpse. They don't want to abuse their corpse."

"Are you saying women worry about how they look after they're dead?"

Rex said, "Women always worry about how they look."

"Can I have one of them doughnuts?" the kid asked. I handed him the bag. There weren't any but cake doughnuts left. "I don't know why they make them things," he said. "Nobody likes 'em."

"Give it here," I said, "I'll eat it."

The kid took a bite and offered me the rest, then busted out laughing.

"Put your seatbelt on," I said.

Rex said, "He's right though, "It's always women who jump. But if they'd seen what I seen, they'd take a bunch of pills, or something."

"Why?" the kid asked.

"You ever seen a body what's hit the water from 300 feet up?"

The kid shook his head.

"Might as well of hit concrete. Nothin' solid left in 'em. They get all crunchy, like a big bag of Fritos. Breaks all their bones. And the drowned ones, they're all swole up and bleached out. Doesn't take but a few hours. Even the niggers. 'Cept some niggers'll turn purple. I don't know why that is."

"You're shittin' me," the kid said.

The fog began to pulse red ahead of us. "There it is." Rex eased over onto the shoulder and pulled up behind a state trooper and a couple of trucks from the parish road crew. The trooper climbed out of his cruiser as we pulled up.

"That's Floyd Foucalt," Rex said.

Floyd was a fat cop with a bad reputation, which was why he mostly worked shit jobs, nights, and weekends. He stretched his arms out over his head, then hitched his gun belt up on his hips and checked his fly. He pulled his hat down low over his eyes and sauntered up to us.

"Hey, Floyd." Rex climbed out of the truck and slammed the door.

"Hey, Rex. Hey, Bill. Who's the kid? Did you bring coffee?"

"Fuckin' rookie," Rex said, handing Floyd the thermos. "What we got?"

Floyd looked the kid up and down. "Do I know you?" he asked.

The kid blushed. "You made me pour out a six pack on the highway a few years back. When I was in high school."

"You sure you're twenty-one?" Floyd asked. "Don't seem like that long ago." Floyd unscrewed the thermos and poured coffee into the cap. "Got damn!" he said, shifting the cup back and forth between his hands. "This thing leakin' or what?"

"Got a crack in it," Rex said. "Drink it fast 'fore it runs out, less you got your own cup."

Floyd held the cup so it wouldn't drip on him and gulped it down the best he could. He spilled some on his shirt, more on his pants, and finally spat out a mouthful and threw the rest away. "How long did you boil these beans, anyhow?"

"Not long," Rex said, "but my socks was in the kettle overnight."

"Fuck your socks."

"Might be the best piece of ass you ever got."

"Or the worst case of crotch rot. Why don't you send that kid after some good coffee?"

"We almost didn't get here," Rex said. "And I wouldn't send that kid round the corner by hisself. Boy could fall off a ladder and be lost 'fore he hit the ground. Send the parish boys if you want."

"You call this fog?" Floyd looked around.

"Had to stop and ask directions of some fella in a rowboat," Rex said, "and he was a good six foot off the ground."

Floyd sighed and pushed back his hat, then scratched his neck behind his ear. "What we got," he said, "is a young woman jumped the bridge last night 'tween midnight and two."

"How'd they know it was a woman?" the kid asked.

Floyd glared at him. "Tommy Flowers run the plates this morning. Car b'long to a girl from LSU. There was folks driving by, but nobody called it in." He shook his head. "Don't know what the world's coming to."

"Why'd she do it?" the kid asked.

We all looked at him.

Floyd hunched his shoulders and said, "Who knows? Maybe she was out drunk driving around. Depressed. Fight with her boyfriend. Maybe she just wanted to kill herself. What difference it make, anyway? How's the missus, Rex?"

"Not so good," Rex replied, and they walked up the bridge past where a disspirited road crew set orange cones on the highway to slow traffic.

* * *

The sun was coming up and I was chilled to the bone from lack of sleep. A foghorn sounded out over the water, and in the distance I could hear a train chumping down the tracks across the river. A bit of a north breeze stirred the fog, and a seagull screeched overhead, though I couldn't see him. The kid was standing around so I hollered at him, "You ain't no tourist, son, get our gear down to the boat. And mind your step. He opened the back gate on the Blazer and took out a steel tool box, a nylon bag that held the pike assembly, and another canvas satchel with a couple of stainless steel grappling hooks and some good nylon line. He slung the bags over his shoulder and lurched off down the road the tool box in his free hand. When he was gone I slipped a flat bottle of Southern Comfort out of my hipboots and took a long swallow, then put my jacket on and slid the bottle into my inside pocket. I grabbed a flashlight and two life preservers, shut the door, and ambled down to the water.

The kid set the gear down on the bank by the dive boat. He was rubbing his elbow.

"Did you fall?" I asked.

"No," he said.

The boat was a zodiac. The crew came upriver a few minutes before we got here and beached it under the bridge. The divers sat off by themselves, their wetsuits on. The crew sat smoking cigarettes and gazing out at the fog.

"Say, Bill?" the kid asked.

"What?" I replied.

"If that girl jumped upriver by Plaquemine, why are we looking for her here?"

"River spits 'em up around here. If they don't hit a snag, that is. They roll along underwater for a while. After a few hours, they bubble up and float to the top. Right past the bridge there's a deep hole, dead water. We find a lot of them here. If we don't find her today, we'll work the banks upstream tomorrow. Better hope we find her today, though."

"Why's that?"

"They're ugly the first day, but by the second or third they get ripe."

A minute later the divers came over and pooh-poohed the water.

"Waste o' time, if you ask me," one said.

"Too damn muddy to see," said the other. He kicked at the ground with his toe.

It was growing light and the breeze combed the fog into tatters, so we glimpsed, from time to time, a boat on the river, or a bit of the far bank. It had rained a lot the past week, and there was a lot of debris in the river besides the usual trash. I could make out a stump bobbing, a barrel, a few planks and boxes. The levee was littered with bottles and cans, plastic buckets, old disposable diapers, whatever kinda shit people throw out. Every now and then the fog lifted enough to see houses and lights in Lutcher on the far bank. There was a rickety-assed pier tilting out into the river with a red light on it. I could see somebody scraping paint off a boat hauled up onto the bank. Then the fog closed in again and I couldn't see past the first truss of the bridge.

Rex and Floyd leaned on the railing above us and looked down, pointing at likely places on the river. There was some traffic now, trucks mostly. The drivers slowed down and gawked as they rumbled over the bridge. I knew the guys from the boat crew, but not too well. They were from Ascension Parish, across the water, and we met up every few years on a drowning, or some kind of training exercise, or to play softball if we got a league up in the summer. "How's Rex's old lady?" one of them asked. "I heard she was sick."

"Not too good," I said. Then I asked the kid to go back and get Rex's thermos and when he was gone I took another sip of whiskey and passed the bottle to the guys in the boat. They took a hit each and then uncorked a bottle of their own and we passed that around. "That's too bad," they said.

Right then Rex whistled and we could see him and Floyd pointing out at something in the water. The crew climbed into the boat, then the divers, grumbling as they lugged their tanks, and I got in last after tossing them the bags with the pike and the grappling hooks. As I kicked the boat off, I looked over my shoulder at the kid running and stumbling down the bank with the thermos. The pilot fired up the motor and in a minute we were bouncing along and I thought it was like riding a rock skipping across the river, only we weren't spinning.

The wind was cold in the boat, the fog made the air heavy and wet, and I was glad I wore my jacket. I tried to make out where Floyd was pointing, but it wasn't much use. Though he hollered, I couldn't make out a word he said over the outboard. I unzipped both bags and rummaged for the radio, but the kid must have stowed it in the toolbox, and I made a mental note to chew his ass when we got back. I screwed the pike shaft and the hook together, out of boredom, mostly.

There was a small searchlight on the front of the boat, and the crewman flicked it on and it fired up with a zap like a flashbulb. It threw out a bright, narrow, orange-ish beam that lit up the fog but didn't show anything on the water. He fooled with it a minute, then shut it off, and we buzzed around in an aimless circle until one of the divers shouted, "Over there!"

The pilot drew us up close, cut the engine, and we coasted slowly towards a pulpy-looking gray shape that floated forlornly just below the surface of the greasy brown river. But up close we saw it was a foam cushion from a couch, with a tattered remnant of blue fabric holding onto one end and fanned out in the water looking, from a distance, like hair. We didn't bother to haul it in. We circled aimlessly until we got hungry, then drank another round of whiskey and headed back to shore.

The kid was still waiting with the thermos. "Where's the radio?" I asked him. He had hung it on his belt. "A lot of good it does me there," I said.

"I thought I was coming." He sounded pouty.

"Don't think, rookie. I carry the radio. I wouldn't trust you to hold your dick. You're here to learn, not to do."

"What am I supposed to learn on the bank?"

"Patience. Why don't you go up and watch the river with Rex?"

"He told me to come down here and help you land the boat."

"Gimme some of that coffee," I said.

"All gone."

"Then take the truck to town and get some more."

"But you said I couldn't drive."

"That was then, this is now. Here's a five," I said, digging in my wallet. "Get coffee and some more of them doughnuts. And make sure the coffee's fresh. If it ain't, tell 'em to brew us up a pot."

After the kid left, Rex came down and squatted down on his haunches, plucked up a dandelion and began to chew on the stem. "Seems like I never get no sleep anymore."

"Myrtle?"

"If it ain't her then it's Francine fighting with that no-good son-in-law of mine."

"I thought they moved to Natchez."

"She come back last weekend. Swears she's gonna quit that sum-bitch forever, but never stays gone more than a week. The little boy cries all the time. Cries at night 'cause he's scared of the dark. Cries in the daytime if you look at him cross-eyed. Wets his pants."

"Somebody been beatin' on him?"

"Could be," Rex said. "If I find out it's so..." his voice trailed off.

"I never could figure out why a woman would stay with a man what mistreats her."

"Beats me," Rex said, then he looked at me and chuckled. "Reckon you'll ever get married again?"

"I'll be paying child support 'til I'm fuckin' near sixty. Why would I want to do that?"

"Pussy?"

"I got more pussy since I was divorced than I ever got from Ellen."

"You musta got at least two good shots?"

"I got at most two good shots, and I don't remember 'em being that good."

"Don't look at me," Rex said, "I didn't sample the merchandise."

"If somebody else can get some off her, more power to 'em."

"How's the kids?"

"They all right."

"They like Lake Charles?"

"Not really."

"They'll get used to it. It's a nice place. Not too far to visit."

"Far enough."

Word came over the radio the girl left a note at home. Said she'd been depressed about school, a boyfriend who left her, some family stuff.

The kid came back with coffee and doughnuts. "Cups," he said, "and napkins, for the messy eaters." He poured coffee all around and then sat down.

Suddenly Rex turned to the kid and asked, "You ever seen a dead body?"

The kid stopped mid doughnut and shook his head.

"The drowned ones get all bloated and pulpy, but they get hard, too, on the inside. Muscles lock up. They'll float face down with their arms dangling, or out to the side, and then they'll lay like that when you haul 'em into the boat. 'Cept the ones what jumped off the big bridge. They ain't nothin' solid left in them. Haul 'em up out of the water and they're like picking up a wet mattress. Dead weight. Like putty."

"Like Gumby and Pokey?" the kid asked.

"What the fuck are you talkin' about? Do you know what he's talkin' about?" Rex looked at me.

I shook my head.

"On TV," the kid said.

"Your mama have any children that lived?" Rex drained his coffee and crumpled his cup. "Gimme a sip of that whiskey, will you?"

I handed him the bottle and he finished it. "Myrtle's got the cancer again," he said.

"I thought it was in remission."

"It was."

"She been to the doctor?"

"Hell, no. I can't get her to go."

"Then how do you know it's back?"

"She's bleedin' again."

"And she won't go? She could get another dose of chemo."

"Says she'd rather die, she was so sick the last time. Says the cure is worse than the disease."

I whistled through my teeth.

Rex looked at the kid. "I had a corpse once sit up in a boat once and spit water. He was a fat boy, too, naked as the day he was born. He was supposed to have been working on some pilot tug. He got drunked-up and went overboard in the middle of the night. That was my rookie year."

"What did you do?" the kid asked.

"I like to shit my pants!" Rex burst out laughing. "I jumped out the boat!"

"No way."

"I did." Rex stood up and stretched. "Like to give me a heart attack. The fellas was just as scared as me. Hell, they all jumped but one. And he was holding the fat boy down and trying keep the boat from tipping over."

"What happened to him?"

"They made him the next chief."

"Not him, the fat boy."

"He died. They'll come to, sometimes, but if they been in the water for long, they's always too fucked-up to live."

Floyd whistled from the bridge and waived. Rex looked, but made no move to get up.

Floyd shouted again, and came towards us on the bridge.

"What's the matter?" the kid hollered. "Got a ten ninety-eight? Fire in the doughnut house?"

"Go see what he wants," Rex told the kid. But just then the radio cackled and Floyd shouted, "Get up, you hunk of shit, there she is!"

Rex and I jumped up, and the crew piled into the zodiac and fired up the outboard. The divers ran over to the bank while I scanned the water and sure enough, there she was, about 200 yards off, just rolling under. Rex waived the divers off and the kid handed me the radio, helped push us off, and in a minute we were just downstream of where we saw her last, but suddenly the girl was nowhere to be seen.

"Shit," Rex said, "where'd she go?"

I raked the water carefully with the pike. I saw a fireman hook a cable once, and it yanked him overboard so hard he dislocated his shoulder. The pilot throttled back to trolling speed. We looped once, then twice, and finally Rex pointed to a flat spot on the water. We covered it twice before I felt the pole snag something heavy.

It was full daylight, now, and the fog was fading fast. The river was brown and smelly like the sewer it is. If everybody in America flushed their toilets simultaneous, New Orleans would flood.

The crew cut the motor and we drifted. I felt for the body, trying to bring her up without setting the hook in her. It ain't fun pulling them out like a dogfish on a gaff. I had to explain once to a distraught grandmother why I'd ripped half her son's face off. And them Catholics like open-casket funerals. I could hear Floyd's voice cracking on the radio in a high pitched frenzy, and then he said, "Pack it up, boys, they found her upriver at White Castle."

Rex shot me a puzzled look, so did the pilot. I swirled my finger in the air, keep circling. I probed the water with the pike.

The radio cracked again and Floyd said, "Come on in, it's almost lunchtime." The rookie shouted from the bank and waived his arms.

"I don't care what Floyd says," I said. "There's a body down there. I saw it."

"Hold on," Rex said into the radio. "Bill thinks he's got one."

"Well, they can't be two bodies, can they?" Floyd said.

"I don't see why not," Rex replied, and right then I got the pole solid under her and levered her up. The crewman reached over and grabbed her by the hair. I reached back to hand the pike to Rex, but he'd turned white, and instead of taking the pike he sat down. Then he passed smooth out—slid down into the bottom of the boat.

She was a pretty little thing, or she would have been if she hadn't taken on so much water. She looked thirteen or fourteen, dirty blonde, in a long blue cotton print skirt, a thin cotton top that didn't come quite past her belly button. There was a strand of beads around one wrist and her feet were bare. I guessed she might have changed her mind and kicked her

Melvin Sterne

shoes off trying to swim. She had her hair in thick ropes like snakes, and a silver ring in her belly button, a tattoo on her right arm I couldn't make out 'cause her skin was bleached.

We laid her on her back in the boat and her eyes were open to the sky. Black water trickled out the corners of her mouth. There was mud and straw on her face, and I couldn't help but brush it away. Her arms reached up like she was asking us for a hand. I covered her with my coat the best I could. Rex groaned, rolled over, and puked.

"You okay?" I asked.

He nodded groggily and wiped his mouth with the back of his hand. "I think I been up too long," he said.

Floyd had hurt his knee climbing down the levee and he lay on the ground swearing while we beached the zodiac. He had us lay the body on the grass while he hobbled around looking stupid. He knelt beside her and checked her dress for pockets, found that she had none, and no panties, either. He tried to read the tattoo on her arm, noted a small gold ring in her nose. "Don't make no sense to me," he said. "Kids these days. When I was growing up the only folks what got tattoos was soldiers and whores, and she don't look like no soldier. You know her?"

I shook my head. "Not that I can recall."

I helped Rex out of the boat. He was wobbly. The kid reached down and touched the dead girl's hair. "Dreadlocks," he said.

"Get off," Floyd growled. "This here's a crime scene, not show and tell."

"Her hair," the kid said. "They call it dreadlocks."

"I call it ugly. Now move on over there outta the way."

"Hey," I said, "get our gear up to the truck." I pointed with my eyes.

The kid looked at me darkly, then turned and took the toolbox up on his shoulder and lumbered up the levee.

Rex bummed a cigarette from one of the boat crew. "You got any whiskey left?" he asked.

They didn't.

"I thought you quit," I said.

"I did. I might quit again. Right now I need a smoke and a whiskey."

The kid skidded back down the levee and disassembled the pike. He wiped the pole sections down with a towel and slipped them into the bag.

"Hey, kid," Rex said, "Drive back into town and get me a quart of Old Granddad and two six packs of Miller tall boys, you hear."

The kid looked at me and I nodded.

"And bring me a pack of Marlboro."

The kid took the gear and a minute later I heard the truck fire up and pull out into traffic.

Floyd was on the radio saying he didn't know where she came from or who she was, but she was dead. An ambulance drove out from town, siren wailing, and a minute later two grim paramedics appeared. They walked slowly down the levee carrying a gurney, which they set by the girl, pulling back the top sheet before stooping beside her and feeling her neck for a pulse. Finding none, they hefted her by her shoulders and feet and plopped her onto the gurney. Then they covered her with the sheet and strapped her in.

"You okay?" I asked Rex.

"I had a fright, that's all."

It was a little past eleven. The traffic on the bridge passed slow as everybody looked to see what the commotion was about. Somebody leaned out a truck window and shouted my name. A meadowlark struck up a song in the pines behind the levee. Swallows darted from under the bridge.

"Kind of pretty here," I said, and Rex nodded. He looked around as though newly aware of his surroundings. The fog had burned away. The crew from Ascension Parish waived and shoved off, the zodiac skipping away over the wake of a passing tug. Beyond the tug the rust-red hull of a freighter loomed, and it sounded a blast from its horn to signal a drawbridge downstream.

"Let's go," Rex said, and I offered him a hand and helped him to his feet. We climbed the levee and stood by the highway. Across the road was a pasture of about eighty acres, with a dozen or so cows grazing, a line of moss-hung live oaks beyond them.

"Myrtle and I was gonna buy a bigger place next year," Rex said. "We was gonna farm some. I was gonna play every weekend, maybe add-on a little recording studio. I can take a full retirement at sixty-two with forty years' service. She ain't but fifty-seven herself." Rex's hand began to tremble. "She started writing me when I was in the war, you know. She was just a kid then, not much older than the girl." He gestured over his shoulder towards the river. "It was some kind of school thing, write a soldier for Christmas. But we wrote a lot after that, and when I came home, I married her."

The paramedics came up the levee and loaded the girl into the ambulance. They drove away quietly.

"I ain't never been with no other girl," Rex said. "I was too scared to fuck the whores in 'Nam, even though they was all over." He laughed, then wiped his eye.

I said, "If the kid don't hurry, we'll have to haul Floyd back up the levee."

"Come on," Rex said, and he grabbed me by the arm and pulled me across the road.

We leaned against the guard rail. A slow tug pushed an oil barge upstream, smoke belching from her stack. I smell burnt diesel.

"For a minute," Rex said, "I thought that was Francine in the water."

"I knew that."

A little red Honda stopped in front of us, the back speakers thumping so the whole car shook. Two teenage girls leaned out the passenger-side windows and waived at us. "What happened?"

"Girl drowned," I replied.

"Oh," they said together. The girl in front seat turned and said something to the others. The girl in the back seat looked sad. "They know who?" she asked.

I shook my head. "Nobody local."

"I thought maybe it was a car wreck," she said. They drove away.

"Did you ever wonder how many bodies float out to the gulf and never get found?" Rex asked.

"No," I said, "Never thought about it."

"There could be a whole boatload of them in the water and we might never know."

I thought about that for a minute. I pictured a river of dead girls, skin bone white, hair like dirty blonde mops, broken arms waiving. Me and Rex and the kid hauling them into a rowboat by the pike as fast as we could, one after another. Our arms ached, sweat rolled down our backs, the boat filled to swamping, but for every one we snagged, ten floated by, their glassy eyes accusing us for letting them slip away. If the fog hadn't lifted, we would've never found this one. "I forgot my jacket," I said.

The kid pulled up in the blazer, leaned across the seat and opened the passenger door. "I brung the whiskey," he said. "I got sandwiches, too. Ya'll hungry?"

"What am I gonna do?" Rex asked. "What am I gonna do now?"

The kid leaned back in the truck and turned the radio on. He had changed the station from Country Cajun to some kind of rap crap out of Baton Rouge. He looked across the highway where Floyd came limping and puffing up the bank. The kid waived, then drummed on the dash with his fingers. "You coming, or what?"

Rex climbed into the back seat and rummaged through the grocery bag. He opened the whiskey and took a slug. "You forgot my cigarettes," he said.

"You shouldn't smoke, anyway," the kid replied. "It's bad for you. You don't want to die of cancer, do you?"

To the south I could see the cranes of a shipyard, and a tall steel railroad drawbridge a few miles downstream, the spans parting to let the freighter through. Somebody sounded their horn at oncoming traffic, and the acid smoke from the tug burned my eyes. The river, almost muddy enough to walk across, rolled endlessly out of sight. I walked around to the driver's side and opened the door. "Scoot over," I said. "I'll drive."

The Heart-Smart Diet

At the trial Alvin's attorney tried to pass the whole thing off as stress brought about by unemployment and a failed marriage. The prosecutor, who campaigned as a hard-liner and vowed to rid Spokane of big-city vice, came out guns blazing. He had all his witnesses in court: the gay tourists from Encino, the girl in the halter-top, the Mini Mart clerk, the Filipino biker-turned-real-estate-developer, the Iranian sculptor, Alvin's soon-to-be-ex-wife, the night manager from the Safeway on Division Street, and the hobo. The city paid big money to fly the gay tourists back from California and put them up at the Downtown Weston. They found the hobo sleeping in a mission in Seattle and had him held as a material witness in the county lockup. It cost the city a small fortune (except for the hobo), but the prosecutor made it clear from the beginning he intended to make an example of Alvin.

Alvin, for his part, looked like he was being made an example of. He shuffled into court wearing an orange jump suit, shackled hand and foot, two armed deputies by his side. The jump suit was a poor fit and Alvin, all five foot seven, a hundred and thirty-six pounds of him, looked more pathetic than dangerous. He smiled weakly at the jury and at his soon-to-be-ex-wife, who narrowed her eyes and then looked away. He sat down at a long table on the left side of the courtroom, next to Ms. Kierney, his court-appointed defense attorney.

Judge Boston entered from a side chamber, the bailiff said, "All rise," and Alvin, Ms. Kierney, the prosecutor, the witnesses, and the jury all rose, then sat when the judge rapped his gavel and said, "The superior court is now in session. Be seated."

Ms. Kierney immediately objected to Alvin's treatment as prejudicial because he had been out on bail until the night before the trial and made no attempt to flee. The judge concurred and the shackles came off, deputies were dispatched back to the police station for Alvin's street clothes. In the mean time, the prosecutor called his first witness, gay tourist number one, to the stand.

Mr. Benchley (sporting a smartly tailored pink suit with wide 1960's-style lapels) recounted the mundane details of the long-anticipated vacation to Banff and Lake Louise that led up to "The events of the evening of November 9th."

Alvin did not recognize Mr. Benchley. When he was arrested, Alvin could not give the police a reason why he was in the parking lot at Spokane Falls. Sitting in court, he vaguely recalled that the night was cool, that the north wind painted his face with the spray from the falls, and that it made little round rainbows in the air circling the halide lights in the parking lot.

The gravel had crunched under Alvin's feet and he remembered that he was cold. He was not wearing a coat and the mist from the falls was almost as bad as rain to stand in. The impulse to steal took Alvin by surprise and he could offer no explanation for his actions. He was over-whelmed by a sudden desire to go home. He had no history of criminal behavior. He had a car of his own, though police found it parked some distance away. He could not recall how he got downtown or how he had spent the afternoon. The prosecutor tried tracing Alvin's whereabouts by credit card records, but Alvin's card's were maxed out and had been cancelled for non-payment. He couldn't have used them even if he wanted. He wasn't drinking—he was sure of that—and he didn't use drugs.

The stick was a matter of opportunity—it was just a broken off pine sapling someone had used for a hiking stick and left leaning against a lamppost. Alvin didn't think the tourists would just give him their car for the asking, and he thought the stick might make him look more menacing. He didn't know the tourists and certainly hadn't "cased" them as the prosecutor suggested. It was dark outside and he didn't even know there were two of them in the car. When Mr. Benchley got out the driver's door Alvin approached him, waived the stick in the air, and shouted, "Give me the keys, asshole!"

On the witness stand Mr. Benchley recalled that he was terrified and forgot where he had put them. "I checked my pockets frantically," he said. When Mr. Karapitachi emerged from the passenger door, Alvin panicked and whacked Mr. Benchley over the head with the stick. Mr. Benchley passed out cold on the spot and remembered nothing until he came to in the ambulance. When asked by the prosecutor he stood up and showed the men and women of the jury the small scar on the top of his head, and the L-shaped scar on the back of his head where he hit the bumper of the

Saab parked in the next spot.

Alvin craned his neck to see—he hadn't seen Mr. Benchley since the incident. There was a line up downtown after Alvin was arrested, but the witnesses were concealed behind a one-way mirror. Alvin was relieved that the damage was no worse than it was. The way Mr. Karapitachi described the event, Alvin expected to see a man with his head misshapen like a deflated soccer ball.

Alvin remembered the weight of the stick in his hand—it was a dry pine sapling but solid, sturdy enough for a good hiking stick—and he remembered the shock of if shearing off when he struck Mr. Benchley. He flatly denied Mr. Karapitachi's claim that he struck Mr. Benchley repeatedly shouting, "Take that you faggot son-of-a-bitch!"

Mr. Karapitachi did not help the prosecution's case when he took the witness stand. He cried continually and mistakenly identified the Bailiff as "That animal." As there were only the two wounds, and no other witnesses, Ms. Kierney moved to dismiss the hate-crime charges of Intimidation and Attempted Murder, and the judge granted the motion.

Alvin remembered Mr. Karapitachi quite clearly. When he saw Mr. Benchley slump to the ground he was so stunned that he likely would have thrown away the stick and run had Mr. Karapitatchi not thrown the keys at Alvin's feet and shouted, "For God's sake, just take the damn thing!" Before Alvin could pick up the keys Mr. Karapitatchi threw him his watch, wallet, and a four-carat diamond ring given him as a "keepsake" by Mr. Benchley. Alvin took the wallet, but not the watch or the ring. The watch was recovered by police at the scene. The ring was never found.

Ms. Kierney moved that the felony theft charges against Alvin be dismissed due to lack of evidence, but the judge was not swayed and declined the motion, ordering that the jury should decide the matter.

Alvin fled the parking lot in Mr. Benchley's 1969 light purple Carmen Ghia (in the police report Mr. Benchley insisted on calling it "fuschia") leaving the hysterical Mr. Karapitachi holding Mr. Benchley's battered head in his lap. Neither Alvin nor the third witness, the girl in the halter-top bikini, could account for the next fifteen minutes. Alvin told the police he panicked as he drove off, took a wrong turn, and got lost.

The girl in the halter-top was walking down highway 2 in Airway Heights when Alvin slowed the stolen Carmen Ghia and pulled alongside her. On the witness stand she swore to tell the truth and said that her name was Miranda Peghram.

The prosecutor smiled sympathetically when she sat down and leaned against the railing in a friendly and informal way. He patted her arm like she was a child and needed reassuring. "How did the defendant look when he pulled up alongside of you on the highway?" he asked.

"He looked a little crazy," Miranda said, stopping to wave shyly at Alvin before answering.

"A little crazy," the prosecutor repeated for emphasis. "And how did you feel when you saw him?"

"At first I was weirded-out," she said.

"Frightened?" asked the prosecutor.

"Yeah, I guess you could say that. I thought he was just another nut case taking me for a whore." Miranda wore a short, navy blue spaghetti-strapped summer dress in court and her hair was cut short and freshly frosted. She pushed it up on her forehead with her left hand whenever the prosecutor asked her a question. She had tattoos on both arms, another on the back of her neck, and one over her left breast. She wore a silver ring in her nose and another in her right eyebrow. Her nails, which Alvin concluded must be artificial, were impossibly long and painted black.

"But you were not engaged in prostitution?" the prosecutor asked.

"Of course not," Miranda replied, pushing up her hair, "This was Airway Heights, not Sprague Street. I was just out for a walk."

When Alvin first saw her she was walking in the direction of oncoming traffic wearing very short cut-off jeans and a green halter-top. Alvin thought she was a prostitute and he slowed down, but then he saw that she was afraid, or disgusted, or both, he started to drive on. He couldn't say why he stopped any more than he could say why he hit Mr. Benchley with a stick and stole his car. He just stopped. "I'm lost," he said. "I'm trying to get to Colville."

Miranda looked the Carmen Ghia over. She checked out the California license plates while she walked around the car. She looked at Alvin—"He looked like a puppydog," she said on the witness stand. Other than needing a shave, he was fairly clean-cut; and if he had got wet from the spray of the falls he had dried out driving around. He wore Levis and a Big Dog sweat shirt. "He looked like your typical lonely married guy out driving around," she recalled. "He looked like a geek. He didn't look like he would hurt a fly." She was the one who asked Alvin for a ride. "I was cold," she explained, "and he seemed like a nice guy. I was going home," she said, nodding her head in the direction of the biker-turned-real-estate-developer, "to Beto's."

Ms. Kierney cross-examined Miranda cruelly. "How many times have you been arrested for prostitution?" she asked, thumbing through a clipboard holding a stack of Miranda's arrest records. "How many aliases have you used? Are you currently on drugs?" The stack was almost an inch thick and Ms. Kierney waived it at the jury for emphasis. She leaned against the railing that fenced the jury off from the rest of the courtroom and looked at Miranda. "And you expect us to believe you?" she asked.

Alvin winced when she said this. Ms. Kierney wore a woman's business suit and she was all business. She was tall and looked smart and slightly mean, cold-blooded. The suit was black with a plain white blouse and Alvin thought she looked like a lady mortician. She was in her early fifties. She wore her hair silver gray and cropped very short. Alvin met her ten minutes before he was arraigned and was going to enter a guilty plea. She told Alvin she put herself through law school after her husband left her. Alvin liked her. Ms. Kierney read the charges and told Alvin to "Sit down and shut up—don't say a word. I'll answer for you."

"Are there any warrants out for you now?" she asked Miranda.

The prosecutor immediately objected and he and Ms. Kierney began arguing loudly. Alvin's attention wandered. He looked at Miranda. He remembered her as sweet and a little vulnerable. "I'm cold" she said, shivering slightly, leaning into Alvin after she climbed into the Carmen Ghia, "can you turn on the heat?" Alvin twisted knobs on the dash at random. He turned on the windshield wipers. He turned them on fast and then he turned them down to intermittent. He finally shut them off. Eventually he found the fan and it blasted out hot air. In a moment they were warm. They drove to north Spokane and somewhere along the way they bought a bottle of Gallo and passed it back and forth.

Miranda looked around the car. She saw Gucci luggage in the back, a plastic trash bag from "Fredericks of Hollywood" hanging on the cigarette lighter, a paper lei dangling from the rear view mirror, and a dancing hula girl glued to the dash. She took a Wham cassette out of the tape player. "This isn't your car, is it?" she asked.

Alvin shook his head and Miranda giggled. "You're just full of surprises," she said. Miranda hopped into the back seat and rifled the suitcases. She emptied everything onto the floor and then took what she wanted and stuffed it into the smaller of the two bags. She took a Nikon camera, two lenses, and a flash. She took a silk blouse. She found a pair of frilly pink women's panties and tried to hang them over Alvin's head, but he almost ran the Carmen Ghia into a ditch. In the bottom of the bag she found a baggie with a bud of Hawaiian pot as big as a turkey leg.

"Jesus Christ!" she shouted when she found the weed. "Will you look at the size of that!" But though she searched the suitcases and contents twice, and the glove compartment, she could not find papers anywhere. "We got to find a Mini Mart," she said.

That was when they ran out of gas. The car sputtered and stopped, Alvin pulled over to the curb. Miranda climbed almost into Alvin's lap and looked at the gauges.

"You stole a car that was out of gas?" she asked incredulously. "This just isn't your day, is it?"

They were in a residential neighborhood and Miranda didn't feel good about it at all. "The first black and white that sees me, I'm gone," she said. "We got to get out of here. Let's high-tail it over to Division Street and I'll call my homey to come pick us up." She climbed into the back seat and slipped on a sweater and a pair of pants she grabbed off the floor. Alvin figured they must have been Mr. Karapitachi's. He was short and closer to Miranda's size. Even so, she had to roll up her sleeves and turn up the cuffs so she wouldn't trip over them. She took the small bag with the camera, the lenses, some clothes, and the pot, and they headed east. "Hold my hand," she said to Alvin. "Try looking like a happy couple and nobody will notice us."

Alvin took Miranda's hand and found it warm and slightly wet. He held it until they reached Division Street and then she shook it loose. It took them fifteen minutes. They found a 7-Eleven and bought a pack of Zig-Zag rolling papers and another bottle of wine. Miranda led Alvin behind the store and pinched off a bud and gave it to him. "I'm gonna make a phone call," she said. "You got any change?" Alvin gave her all the change in his pocket and sat down by the dumpster with his back against the wall. He tried to roll a joint, but he hadn't smoked pot since he was in college and he botched it badly. It was fat and loose in the middle, bent at one end, and the paper came unglued on the other.

Miranda came back from the phone booth. He handed her the joint. "What in the hell is this?" she asked, just before it fell apart completely.

Alvin looked down and said nothing.

"Don't you know this shit is expensive?" Miranda asked, and Alvin shook his head. "Well it is," she said. She took out the pot and sniffed the bag. "And this shit looks like dynamite, too. Look at the hair in that bud." Alvin leaned over and looked while Miranda rolled an expert joint with one hand—tight and smooth as a cigarette. She slipped it into her mouth and drew it out wet with a sucking motion. Alvin blushed and Miranda smiled.

"Are you married?" Miranda asked.

"No," Alvin said.

Miranda eyed the white patch on Alvin's ring finger.

"We're getting a divorce," he said. "She left me."

"I'm sorry to hear that," she said. "How long were you together?"

"Twelve years."

"That's a long time."

"We met in high school."

Miranda lit the joint and inhaled. She tried to hold the smoke in but couldn't and let it out in a fit of coughing. She handed the joint to Alvin and gasped, "Expando."

Alvin took a cautious toke and also choked, though not as badly as Miranda. After a moment he said, "For a sculptor."

"A what?" Miranda asked.

"A sculptor."

"That's too bad."

"They met at a charity auction."

"I hate shit like that," Miranda said. She passed the joint back to Alvin.

Alvin held it in his hand and wondered whether she meant infidelity or charity auctions. He decided that she must mean the auctions. "I came home and they were sitting on the couch. They had a restraining order."

"The fuckers."

"I had to pack my clothes and move into a hotel."

"Life's tough," Miranda said, taking a sip of wine. "Any kids?"

Alvin shook his head.

"That's good."

"We tried for years. She said I shot blanks, but when we went to the doctor he said her fallopian tubes were knotted up. Do you think if we'd had kids it might have helped?" Miranda shrugged her shoulders. "Sometimes. Then again, sometimes kids are just something else to fight about."

"Do you have any kids?" Alvin asked.

Miranda sucked the joint down to the nub and then threw it away.

She exhaled the smoke in a dense blue cloud and watched it drift away. "C'mon," she said, "let's get out of here."

On the witness stand Miranda told a different story. She left out the part about stealing the camera and finding the pot, and when they got to the Mini Mart she said Alvin stole the clerk's car keys from his coat pocket even though she did it. She fidgeted in her chair, crossed and uncrossed her legs frequently. Her testimony ended when the sheriff's deputies returned with Alvin's clothes, and the judge ordered a recess while he changed. When the hearing resumed, the Mini Mart clerk took the stand.

The Mini Mart clerk said his name was Bell. He stood average height, but weighed close to 250 pounds. His arms looked as thick as tree stumps and his face was covered with a bushy black beard that hung down almost to his belly button. He wore black leather motorcycle pants and a Harley Davidson tee shirt. The night Alvin and Miranda came into the Mini Mart, Bell was wearing a leather vest and blue bandana, but other than that he was dressed just the same.

The judge, the prosecutor, and Alvin's attorney huddled together for about five minutes when Bell gave his name. He said his name was "Bell. Just Bell. No first name. No last name. Just Bell." Ms. Kierney wanted him barred from the stand but the judge said that there was no precedent to bar people with unusual names from testifying and he wanted to hear what Bell had to say, so they let him continue.

Bell pointed to Alvin and said that Alvin had asked to use the bathroom, which was in back in the storeroom, and not generally open to the public. He said that Alvin didn't look like a thief and so he made an exception out of "The kindness of my heart." Alvin, he said, must have taken the keys out of his jacket, which hung on a nail by the back door. What he didn't mention was that Miranda sweet-talked the clerk into the back room to smoke a joint.

Alvin was, by that time, stoned out of his mind, and didn't smoke anymore, although he did help himself to a warm six pack of carbonated wine. He paced back and forth while Miranda and Bell talked like old friends. He read the labels on the pints of ice cream in the freezer, and then sat down and watched the store on the black and white security camera.

Miranda gave Bell a phony telephone number and explained that it was a numeric pager and that if Bell called she would call him right back. She surprised Alvin outside when she flashed the keys to Bell's truck and asked if Alvin wanted to drive.

The truck was easy to spot—there was no mistaking it was Bell's. It was a jacked-up '69 Ford 4 x 4 painted battleship gray with a Harley Davidson decal in the rear window and silver mud flap girls hung behind monster, oversized tires. There was a bumper sticker that read "Carnivores Eat More Pussy" on the right side, and another one that read, "You Can Have My Gun When You Pry My Cold Dead Fingers from Around the Trigger" on the left. Miranda rifled the glove compartment and found a stubby, chrome-plated .357 magnum, which she packed in the small suitcase along with the pot and the camera and the clothes and the lenses.

Alvin knew it was a bad idea to drive, stoned as he was, but he didn't say so at the time. The truck fired right up. The engine roared loud as the Fourth of July, and they peeled-out in a thick cloud of exhaust and burnt rubber before Bell ran out into the parking lot after them.

Bell valued the truck at about $15,000, a figure Ms. Kierney vigorously disputed. "It was mostly my time," Bell said, folding his arms obstinately and glaring across the room at Alvin. "Do you have any idea how many hours I put in that thing? I value that truck right next to my bike and my wife."

The police found the truck in a ravine where Alvin and Miranda left it after Alvin ran off the road. The accident wasn't as bad as it looked even though the truck was a total loss. The slide down was broken by a stand of young pines that the truck sheared off, one after another, until they hit bottom and wrapped the truck around an old cottonwood that didn't give an inch. Alvin cut his lip on the steering wheel. Miranda screamed the whole way but wasn't hurt at all. When they climbed out of the truck Miranda laughed so hard she had to sit down. "You're just a natural-born car thief," she said, slapping her knees and rolling on the ground.

The bottom of the ravine was sandy and dry. Alvin sat down on the suitcase beside her. Miranda composed herself and they sat quietly for a while before she rolled another joint. They smoked it, finished the wine, and at length set out for Beto's house. Alvin felt husbandly guilt for causing the accident and offered to carry Miranda's bag. They trudged along in the dark and managed well enough—the ravine was close to Beto's house and Miranda had walked it before, though never at night. They crossed the creek twice and Alvin missed the stepping stones both times. His filled his shoes with water and they squeaked after that with every step. His feet turned numb with cold almost immediately.

"There's nothing worse than walking with cold feet," Miranda said, and Alvin agreed.

Ms. Kierney had only one question for Bell—what had become of the security tape? Bell replied that the tape, which he meant to save, had been accidentally erased.

Ms. Kierney scowled and lobbied the jury hard that Bell's credibility was suspect at best. Alvin watched them closely, hoping for a positive sign, but they seemed to react with bored indifference. He had, after all, stolen the Carmen Ghia, and his fingerprints were all over the driver's side of Bell's truck. Who stole the keys, and how, seemed, in retrospect, a moot point.

Beto Maldonado took the stand next. He wore a handsome blue suit with a white shirt and red tie, a white silk handkerchief peeking out of his breast pocket. Except for his Fu Manchu moustache and long, black, braided ponytail, he looked just like a real estate developer. And he was a real estate developer, of sorts, although he had had numerous run-ins with the city over land-use issues. He had inherited a section of land from his grandfather that included the ravine where Alvin crashed Bell's truck. The area was dotted with houses built by Beto or on land Beto parceled out. Beto nodded and smiled at the jury, and seemed to be on good terms with the prosecutor, greeting him by his first name. Miranda was not his girlfriend, he said, but sometimes "Crashed on his couch." It was his way of trying to help her get on her feet in troubled times, Beto said. He cited several charitable organizations he supported.

Alvin, of course, knew otherwise. Beto wasn't home when he and Miranda emerged from the woods, but she knew where a spare key was hidden—in the drainpipe—and let them in through the back door. Alvin sat on the couch in the recreation room rubbing his toes while Miranda took a shower and changed clothes. She came downstairs in a green miniskirt with a white sweatshirt, a towel wrapped around her head. She put on a ZZ Top CD and she and Alvin smoked another joint and waited for Beto to come home. When she heard the front door open, Miranda rushed down the hall to greet him. They came into the rec room arm-in-arm and she introduced Alvin, though Beto did not seem very happy to meet him.

Beto testified that he did not know about the accident until the police spotted the truck the next morning and came around asking questions. This part was true—Miranda warned Alvin that Beto had a "short fuse" and that they were probably better off if he never heard about it.

From the moment they arrived at Beto's house, Alvin sensed a change in Miranda. He suspected it was just a matter of time until he was the odd man out. The suitcase with the pot, the camera, and the gun had disappeared. Miranda found more wine in the fridge but poured Alvin a glass, whereas before they had shared the bottle.

While Miranda cuddled up on the couch with Beto and placated him with a joint, Alvin pondered his options. When he saw that Miranda was not wearing panties under her miniskirt, he knew that he had none. He slipped on his shoes but left his socks, still wet, balled up under the couch. Beto led Alvin to the front door and pointed out the road that wound up the ravine and back to the highway. As soon as Alvin stepped off the porch Beto closed the door and turned off the light. Alvin heard the deadbolt slide into place with a solid click.

Alvin stood in the front yard shivering. He decided he would go back and ask if he could borrow some socks and perhaps a sweater. He knocked on the door and paused, but there was no answer so he tried the bell. After waiting on the porch for about five minutes, Alvin slipped around to the back of the house, where he peered in a window and watched Miranda giving Beto a blow job. Either she or Beto had removed her sweatshirt, and Alvin thought that Miranda was really quite pretty, and watched the proceedings with considerable interest.

Beto told a very different story to the jury—painting a picture of Alvin as drunk and belligerent, refusing his offer of a cab and having to be told three times to leave. Miranda, he said, was exhausted from her travails, and fell asleep on the couch as soon as Alvin was gone.

Alvin sought out Miranda in the room and recalled fondly the way she looked, the way her breasts bounced and swayed while she hunkered down on Beto's cock. When they made eye contact Miranda looked away.

After a while, Beto led Miranda upstairs. Alvin waited for a while, then took the spare key from the drainpipe and let himself in. He took Miranda's sweatshirt off the floor and put it on. That warmed him up, but he found that he was ravenously hungry, so he poked around the kitchen until he found a jar of pepperoni sticks. He ate several—they were salty as hell—and when he was full he stuffed the rest in his pocket.

Next to the kitchen was the laundry room, and Alvin found a hamper and a pair of dry socks. The prosecutor had the socks in a plastic bag and he showed them to the jury. The socks didn't match and the jury snickered at the sight, but it was dark and Alvin, having no more experience as a burglar than he had as a car thief, thought it best not to turn on a light.

There was another door leading from the laundry room. Alvin opened the door and found the garage, with Beto's collection of motorcycles all shiny and lined up in a row, keys in the ignition. Alvin told the police he intended to return the bike—but his credibility had hit rock bottom. He found the electric garage door opener and was out of sight before Beto could run downstairs.

"It was five minutes past nine," Beto said. "There was a clock in the hallway, and another in the kitchen by the phone." The police dispatcher showed the call coming in at 9:15, but no one considered the difference significant. Of course, by the time officers arrived to take a report, Miranda was gone, as was the suitcase with the camera, the lenses, the clothes, the pot, and the chrome-plated .357 magnum. Even if the police had known to look for them, they were nowhere to be found. Now, of course, it was his word against theirs.

Alvin's soon-to-be-ex-wife, Felicia, was in the courtroom. She took the day off from her job as branch manager for the Aluminum Workers Credit Union. Alvin sensed that she would like to testify against him, but by quirk of Washington law, she could not be called by the prosecution to testify against Alvin as long as they were married. Alvin, of course, could have called her, but Ms. Kierney decided not to risk it. So Felicia sat next to her sculptor boyfriend, Ibram, and alternated listening to the testimony with reading a romance novel.

Alvin hated Ibram long before the day he came home and found Ibram sitting on Alvin's couch wearing Alvin's slippers and with his arm around Alvin's wife. They had actually all met several times in the year before Ibram started up the affair with Felicia. They ran in the same social circles, but especially the charity art auction put on every year by the Artists in Motion Society (AIMS) to Feed the Homeless. Apparently Ibrim and Felicia met at the 1999 AIMS auction and by the time they reached the planning stages for the 2000 auction their romance was in full swing and they spent more time planning their elopement than the event.

Alvin described Ibrim as a "loser"—meaning he had quit his day job to live in a run-down trailer in the boonies where he welded junk and old car parts into statues of monsters. There is no accounting for tastes, however, and Ibrim's work had suddenly become wildly popular. He basked shamelessly in his moment in the sun, appearing on local TV, donating art to the charity auction, even teaching a class at the Spokane Community College.

Felicia thought he was the hottest thing since French toast but Alvin didn't put two-and-two together until he came home and they threw him out. They had restraining orders drawn up and a property settlement outlined that included receipts and cancelled checks. They had set Alvin up. As he explained to Ms. Kierney, he felt like he was, "Down ten runs in the ninth inning before he knew he was at the ballpark."

Ibrim looked his usual immaculate self as the bailiff swore him in. He was tall, black-haired, and handsome; dressed in a gray suit with a forest green shirt and royal blue tie. He adjusted his tie before taking his seat, and Alvin saw the sparkle of diamonds cufflinks in the light. They were his diamond cufflinks—Alvin was sure of it—given to him by Felicia on their first anniversary. But he seldom wore them, so he saw no reason to make a fuss about it. Felicia was probably glad to see Ibrim wear them. She complained constantly about Alvin's appearance. You've gained weight, Alvin. You look like a slob, Alvin. You're going nowhere, Alvin. Maybe she was right.

Ibrim would like to have talked about Alvin all day but the defense objected and the judge made it clear that anything Ibrim heard from Felicia was hearsay and not admissible as evidence. In the end, he confined his testimony to just one thing.

Alvin closed his eyes and remembered the roar of the bike underneath him as he thundered down the road. The wind tore through his clothes and his eyes streamed with wind-blown tears. He had ridden smaller bikes before, but nothing like the big Harley, and its power left him breathless, adrenalized. He did not remember that it was the night of the auction until he passed the civic center downtown and saw the advertisement on the Marquee. The same impulse that led him to steal the Carmen Ghia urged him to ride the bike inside, right out onto the dance floor, pausing only long enough to let the automatic doors at the entry open ahead of him.

Once inside there was no stopping him and he circled the room scattering art patrons in all directions, upsetting tables of hor d'ourves, knocking down statuary and shattering glass and ceramic exhibits until he spied Ibrim and Felicia. Alvin didn't lay the bike down intentionally. It was really just too much bike for him to handle, especially on a polished marble floor. But he did lay it down, and in style, taking out the multi-tiered cake that was the centerpiece of the event, and the bleachers built for the orchestra. He emerged from the wreck unscathed.

One of the guests had brought a video camera and had the presence of mind to record the whole thing. The prosecutor interrupted Ibrim's testimony to introduce the tape as evidence and they showed it to the court via closed circuit TV. Alvin couldn't keep from laughing, nor could the jurors. At the end of the tape he and Ibrim stood fact-to-face. Alvin realized he had put Carmela's sweatshirt on backwards, and he had lost a shoe in the accident.

"What did the accused say to you?" the prosecutor asked Ibrim, stopping the video tape as it zoomed in on Alvin's face.

Alvin could not remember what he said, and he leaned forward in his seat to hear Ibrim's reply. He looked at the face on the TV screen and felt a curious detachment from the man he saw. There was a similarity on the outside, but it felt, to Alvin, something like looking at seashells on the beach.

When Alvin was a boy his parents took him to Moclips every summer, to a cabin they owned on the Washington coast. The shore was rocky and the water cold. Alvin would walk for hours barefooted on the rocks, mindful of the barnacles. He carried an old tin bucket and he filled it with shells, crabs, starfish to dry in the sun, and errant floats that washed ashore from the fishing boats that set their nets along the bay.

Alvin's father taught him the types of clams that could be dug from the sand or found in the water. Some were edible, some were not, and there were ways to tell one species from another. "But how do the clams recognize each other?" Alvin asked.

That's how he felt in court, leaning forward, waiting to hear what his wife's soon-to-be-next-husband would say about him. The face on the TV screen looked like him, talked like him, perhaps even occupied the same space and time that he had, but it was just a shell. Alvin did know who he was.

Ibrim cleared his throat and said, "I remember exactly what he said. It was so darned peculiar." Ibrim's voice stumbled over the word darned, as though he had almost said damned, but caught himself just in time. "He said, 'Do you believe everybody has somebody out there just for them?'"

The prosecutor thought about this for a moment. "And what did you answer?" he asked.

"I said that I did."

"And did the accused reply?"

"He said, 'Well there isn't. Not for me, anyway.'"

Alvin was sure that this was true and he wondered if the jury would acquit him on the basis of this fact alone. He was surprised when Ms. Kierney cross-examined Ibrim and asked if he thought this was a rational thing for a man who had just rode into a charity ball on a stolen motorcycle to say. But the prosecutor immediately objected and the judge sustained the objection saying, "That's not a conclusion the witness is qualified to draw. Counsel may call its own expert to interpret the testimony, if she pleases."

Alvin did not remember hitting Ibrim, or fleeing the civic center, and he had no explanation for why he went back to the Safeway where he used to work. It had been six months since they had fired him. When the police pressed him on this point he shrugged his shoulders and said, "Maybe I was hungry. It's no crime to be hungry."

The next witness was the little hobo who told the judge his name was, "Cannonball Bob" and was promptly objected to by Ms. Kierney. The judge rolled his eyes, and consulted the arrest report and transfer papers from the King County jail in Seattle. Cannonball Bob, who sported a stiff new pair of blue denim coveralls and a yellow tee shirt, had been staying at the Union Gospel Mission downtown under the name of Bob Kennedy. He gave that name when the Seattle Police picked him up and hadn't objected to using it then. He would have to own up to it, or the judge would hold him in contempt. Muttering that it wasn't fair, Bob took his oath and was seated, but folded his arms across his chest and refused to answer any of the prosecutor's questions.

When the prosecutor complained and asked the judge to hold the Bob in contempt, the judge laughed out loud and said, "Bill, he's your witness. You brought him here. If he won't talk that's hardly my problem."

The prosecutor then showed a grainy black and white security tape from the store that clearly showed Alvin and the hobo walking in the aisle of the frozen food department. They stopped in front of a display and Alvin opened it. He took out a stack of boxes—it was hard to see how many there were, but he handed them to Cannonball Bob and waived goodbye as Bob walked out of the store. A minute later the video showed store personnel rushing out the door, but they returned empty-handed. Alvin, meanwhile, had busied himself tidying up the display, and he kept at it until the police came in and arrested him.

"Did the accused say anything to you?" the prosecutor asked Bob.

Bob looked at Alvin and winked. He had a kindly face, wrinkled, but wrinkled in a good way, with laugh lines around his eyes extending up and across his cheeks from the corners of his mouth. He had a new growth of gray whiskers, though when Alvin saw him in the store he wore a full beard that looked almost white. Alvin smiled back at him and Bob looked back at the prosecutor. "I don't remember," he said.

Alvin remembered what he said. It was only a mile from the civic center to the Safeway where he had been the frozen foods manager. It was the shittiest job in the store and everybody knew it. They gave you gloves to keep your hands warm, but they didn't work for beans. You couldn't grip the boxes with your gloves on so you took them off until your hands froze stiff, and then you put the gloves back on again. And marketing was forever coming up with specials and new ideas so that you spent half your time shuffling stock from one freezer to another. It was repetitious work—taking individual boxes out of cartons and stacking them into displays; moving up and down, back and forth. Your wrists and fingers swelled and your back and elbows ached. Alvin couldn't keep a crew. They transferred, quit, got hurt, or called in sick. That was, he thought, why they sacked him. It was why they sacked the guy before him, and probably why they would sack the guy that followed him. Alvin worked that job for seven years, and since he had been fired he had been reduced to day labor. If anybody could make a living as a frozen foods manager, Alvin thought, they ought to be next in line for Chairman of the Board.

The little hobo was sitting on the curb outside the store when Alvin came along. Alvin had thrown away his remaining shoe, his sweater was still on backwards, and he wore different colored socks, but if he looked strange the hobo didn't say a word. "Got a light?" he asked, but Alvin did not have one.

The hobo asked Alvin if he had any spare change and Alvin fished around in his pockets and found that he did not.

"That's too bad," the little hobo said.

"Yeah," Alvin said, and then, after a minute, he added: "I sure could use a drink."

"I don't drink," the hobo said, and this surprised Alvin. "Well, I guess I do drink," he said, "but I try not to. I break out in spots when I drink."

"In spots?" Alvin asked. He imagined the little hobo painted up like a leopard. "What kind of spots?"

"Spots like Dallas, New Orleans, Philly, Chicago, Denver, and Cheyenne. Actually, I've only been drunk twice in my life."

"Twice?" Alvin said.

"Yeah," the hobo said, "From 1967 'til 1989, and from 1992 until last week." The hobo laughed, but Alvin didn't get the joke.

The hobo looked down and played with his shoelaces absent-mindedly.

They were black work boots, and Alvin remembered that were well-worn. He looked up at the witness stand and saw that Cannonball had got some new boots since then. Brown ones, and leather, but not so worn as the others.

"Why'd you quit?" Alvin asked.

"I got religion." There was another long pause, and then the hobo said, "Hell, I ain't no good liar. I went to prison."

"Last week?" asked Alvin.

"No. In '89. I was on a drunk and robbed a bank in a black out. I might have got away with it but I took a cab. I didn't mean no harm. I was just drunk and didn't know what I was doin'."

"I know what you mean." Alvin still had the pepperoni sticks in his pocket. He took one out and offered one to the hobo, but the hobo declined saying: "No thank you, I'm on a diet."

The hobo didn't look too fat to Alvin. "What kind of diet?" Alvin asked.

"For my heart. Ticker's starting to miss a beat every now and then. The doctor give me these." The hobo pulled a little brown vial out of his pocket. He opened the bottle and shook out a couple of tiny blue pills into his palm. "You want one?" he asked, holding his hand out to Alvin. Alvin shook his head, and the hobo swallowed the pills dry. The hobo sighed, thumped his left breast twice with his fist, then reached in his pocket and pulled out a rumpled piece of paper. "He give me this, too," he said, and Alvin took the paper and held it up to the light to read.

The paper was headed The Heart-Smart Diet and listed foods to eat and foods to avoid. Alvin knew a little about the four food groups and the food pyramid. The paper was liberally illustrated and it occurred to Alvin that it was likely written for illiterates. He skipped to the bottom of the page and saw the address of the Kootenai County Health Department.

"Idaho?" Alvin asked.

"Yeah," the hobo said. "Last thing I remember I was sittin' on the western flyer and had a dizzy spell. I woke up in hospital in Coeur d'Alene. I'm s'posed to be there yet, but I get restless if I stay inside too long."

"I hear that," Alvin said.

"I been travelling for nigh fifty years."

"You ever been married?" Alvin asked.

"No," the hobo said. "I had me some girlfriends, but I never figured I was the marrying type."

"I used to think I was," Alvin said, "but now I'm not so sure."

"Don't take to the road, son," the hobo said, patting Alvin on the shoulder. "She's the most jealous lover there is. Once you start you can't stop. If you try to settle down she'll whisper in your ear until she drives you crazy. Then you pack it up with no thought a'tall about nobody else, and just head out again. It's purdy sometimes—I admit to that—but it's cold and lonesome too. Whatever you're thinking, you'd best just hang around a little longer until you work things out."

Alvin nodded. A family pulled up in a green mini-van and got out, a husband and wife with a little boy in tow. The boy pointed at Alvin and the hobo as they walked by and said "Damn beggars." His mother gave the boy's arm a shake.

The hobo sighed. "I shore am hungry. I was hoping somebody might gimme a dollar so I kin get something to eat."

Alvin stood up. "Come on," he said, "I can fix you up."

Alvin led the hobo inside and down the frozen food aisle. "Look here," he said, smiling proudly and pointing at a rack of frozen dinner trays. Alvin opened the case and took out a half-dozen boxes. He didn't think about how or where the hobo might cook them. He took them out of the case and stacked them in the hobo's hands.

The hobo read the label and Alvin pointed at the little logo printed on the corner of the box. "Heart Smart," the Hobo said. "Well I'll be damned."

"Go on," Alvin said. "I'll cover you."

The hobo looked around skeptically.

"It's okay. I used to work here. They won't give you any trouble. There's only one checker in front and she can't leave the register.

Everybody else is stocking shelves or out back unloading trucks. You just walk right out the door and keep going. By the time anybody comes after you, you'll be off the parking lot, and once you're off company property, nobody can touch you. Company policy. I swear." Alvin raised his right arm. "Scout's honor."

"Thank you," the hobo said, clutching the boxes tightly. He looked over his shoulder once as he headed for the door.

Alvin waived. When the hobo was gone Alvin muttered under his breath, "And thank you for shopping at Safeway."

After that Alvin looked at the shelves and sighed. They were in a sad state, and he knew his replacement was not up to the task. He opened the case and tidied up the stacks of Heart Smart dinners, then he started on the frozen vegetables medleys. By the time the police arrived, Alvin had worked his way down to the desert section.

The hobo was excused from the stand and the Safeway night manager took his place. He knew Alvin. They had worked together for a while at another store a few years before. "I always thought Alvin was a little weird," he said. He described Alvin's job performance saying, "He was in way over his head."

"Was he vindictive?" the prosecutor asked.

"Likely so," the night manager replied.

Ms. Kierney called only one witness, a pale young psychologist just out of college. Debbie talked at length about fugue states and post traumatic stress disorder. "It was possible," she said, "for a person to reach an emotional overload and trip the breaker, so to speak."

"What would that look like?" Ms. Kierney asked, but Alvin was not listening anymore. He took out a piece of paper he carried in his pocket and began to read. It was the diet sheet from the Kootenai County Health Department, the one labeled "The Heart Smart Diet." Surely, he thought, this was given to me for a reason. Alvin read the list again and wondered what was the magic combination; the foods themselves or the preparation, the combinations of diet and exercise, meditation, or medication. There must be something, he thought, that might make him want to live again, that could mend his broken heart.

The Funeral

The morning of the funeral Mama Kay dressed Tyler in a black shirt and charcoal-gray wool-tweed jacket she bought the day before at the Saint Vincent de Paul's thrift store in Tifton. The shirt was too big and missed a button on the right cuff. Tyler complained, but Mama Kay didn't have time to fix it so she fastened the cuff with a safety pin. The jacket was too short in the sleeves, too, but there was nothing Mama Kay could do about that. She told Tyler to keep his arms by his side and nobody would notice. Mama Kay fussed over him like he was getting his school picture taken, and even slicked his hair down with some of his father's Brylcream, but all Tyler could think about was that Daddy Frank would say it was a sin to buy from Catholics. When Mama Kay was done with him he stood in front of the mirror scratching his neck where the wool "itched" him, and moving his arms this way and that, watching the sleeves ride up and down, and looking to see if the safety pin showed.

"You look fine, darlin'," Mama Kay called from the bathroom, where she was putting on her makeup.

The mirror was hung on Tyler's closet door. It was old, and some of the silver coating behind the glass was gone. Tyler messed with it and found that if he opened the door just right, he could see Mama Kay's reflection in the bathroom mirror. She was bent over the sink. She wore a low-cut black slip over a matching lacy bra and bikini panties. The pale light of the bathroom's single sixty-watt bulb made the vee of her cleavage yawn like a cave. Mama Kay never put on her dress until the last thing, lest she show sweat lines under her arms.

His sister Jane, who was about to turn fourteen, got a black widow's dress and a veil, which made her look grown-up and somber, even if she was flat-chested and skinny as a bean pole. Folks said Jane was stupid because she didn't talk much—she had been held back twice in school already. When Tyler came out into the hall Jane was standing on one leg with a far-off look in her eyes.

"Hey," he said, and Jane smiled and nodded, swaying a little bit back and forth.

Mama Kay was not their real mother. Tyler's real mother ran off to Alabama with a Baptist preacher from a church downtown. Tyler's father brought Mama Kay home from the Crossroads Tavern shortly after Tyler's real mama ran off. She was taller than Daddy Frank, blonde, with something called full hips, which meant not fat, but not skinny either. Sometimes she dyed her hair platinum, and folks said she looked just like Marilyn Monroe. She was a war widow and had a black dress in the closet from when her first husband died. Mama Kay forgot to air it out the night before so it smelled of moth balls, but before they left for church Mama Kay sprayed on so much perfume nobody could stand to sit next to her anyway. She stood in the hallway and did a little shimmy pulling her dress over her shoulders and down her hips. She knelt down and Tyler zipped up the back for her.

They piled into Daddy Frank's old Dodge pickup, which was the only thing he left them that was worth anything. Jane rode shotgun, with the stick shift sticking up between her legs. Her dress hitched up way above her knees and Mama Kay slipped it down some and reminded Jane to, "Be decent. Act like a lady." Jane had taken to lifting her skirt up and looking at herself lately in the most uncomely manner and in the most inconvenient places, like church, or the grocery store. Tyler played with the glove compartment until the handle fell off, and then found that it would not stay shut, and Mama Kay scolded him all the way to town for pestering her.

They drove to the Pentecostal Church, which was on the edge of town, rather than to the Baptist Church, which was downtown between city hall and the Dairy Queen. Tyler preferred the Baptist church and the social life it afforded him after services. Daddy Frank had been born and raised a Baptist, but in the last few years had switched to the Holy Rollers, not so much because he held with talking in tongues, but because the Pentecostals were "plain folk" who didn't believe in "puttin' on airs." It didn't help any that it was the preacher from this same church who ran off with Tyler's real mama. The recentness of his involvement with the Pentecostals may have contributed to the small turnout at the funeral— there being only a dozen or so mourners present. That and the fact that Tyler's daddy was what townsfolk called a "mean drunk." There weren't hardly any flowers, and the coffin was closed.

Tyler knew what people said behind his daddy's back. They

whispered in the aisles of grocery stores and nodded in his direction when he walked downtown. One Saturday morning, when Tyler rode his bike past the Crossroads Tavern, two men in the parking lot whistled at him and said, "Hey Tyler! Hoo, boy! Your daddy sure is one tough-ass cuss." Tyler wasn't quite sure how to take that.

Tyler spent plenty of Saturday mornings riding his bike around town, looking for Daddy Frank's truck (if Daddy Frank came home without it on Friday night) or Daddy Frank (if he had not come home at all). That particular time was one of the had-nots. Tyler never did find his father, though eventually Daddy Frank called from Dougherty County jail asking for bail money. They found his truck in the ditch on highway 82 the other side of Albany. Daddy Frank had got drunk at The Crossroads and pistol-whipped two locals who made a joke about a preacher running off with some fella's wife. He had no recollection of it, but he told the state troopers who pulled him over that he was on his way to Alabama to "shoot that self-righteous son-of-a-bitch." He spent thirty days on a county road crew. Mama Kay, Tyler, and Jane got to visit him sometimes, and they brought the whole gang cornbread and lemonade when they did.

At the funeral, they passed around a picture of Daddy Frank in a sailor's uniform and another one of him with the semi he drove for the Valley Grower's Association. In both of these pictures he was smiling—a big-boned round-faced man with close-cropped blond hair, a long red scar running from his left cheekbone to his chin, his arms pale blue with tattoos. Mama Kay dabbed her eyes and sniffed through the sermon. The preacher said a few words about heaven and hell and the importance of giving your life to Jesus. Tyler heard a woman behind them whisper, "He was not drunk. He was up three days on pep pills and fell asleep at the wheel. Ran head-on into the abutment." The man she whispered to whispered back, "Took 'em two hours to cut him out, him crying and moaning the whole time. Then he died on the way to the hospital. I heard his last words were, 'Can I get a beer on the way?'"

When it was over they sang "Amazing Grace" and a song called "Big Bad John" which had been Daddy Frank's favorite. Then they got in their cars and followed the hearse to the cemetery and buried him. The pallbearers lowered the coffin into the ground and his mama pitched a rose and a handful of dirt after it. A man in a VFW uniform played 'taps' on the bugle. He played very badly, and Tyler felt sorry for him. Tyler saw Jane lift her skirt and look at herself again, and Mama Kay shook her arm to make her stop.

At the far end of the cemetery an old black man sat in the shade of an oak tree smoking a pipe, a shovel on the ground at his feet. He wore overalls and a red and white checkered shirt, and Tyler watched as he slipped a flask out of his pocket and tipped it back and drank. Tyler waved and the old man waved back. As they turned to go, a covey of quail took flight from a bean field across the road, their wings beating the air like a drum roll.

At home Mama Kay had planned a picnic and invited everybody she knew to come. "It's what he would have wanted," she explained. Mama Kay wore her black dress and veil, but Tyler changed into jeans and Jane into slacks. Tyler was hoping some of his friends would come over and they could play baseball, but none did, so he rode his bike along the river until he got hungry.

The ladies from the church brought fried chicken enough for a small army and someone baked a ham for sandwiches. Mama Kay made lemonade and iced tea with mint leaves in it, and a pound cake for desert. Tyler snuck a Co-Cola from the fridge and shared it with Jane behind the house. Mama Kay spread a tablecloth on the ground, and he and Jane ate quietly while the adults sat at the picnic table. Jane nibbled on a chicken wing. Tyler listened to the adults talking.

"I suppose I will get some kind of a widow's pension from the state or something," Mama Kay said. "I believe I can collect Frank's GI bill, too."

"Who's GI Bill?" Jane asked.

Tyler shrugged. "Must be a friend of daddy's," he said.

"Is Daddy Frank coming back?"

Tyler shook his head.

Jane smiled.

A shiny new white Cadillac pulled up in front of their house and a man and two women got out. Tyler craned his neck to see who they were, but he didn't know them. A good-looking woman in a knee-length blue dress ran right up to Mama Kay and they hugged in the front yard. "I'm so happy to see you," the woman said. She put heavy emphasis on the "see."

"I'm so glad you came, Mindy," Mama Kay replied. "I wasn't sure you would make it."

"Of course, I just wish it could be under pleasanter circumstances,"

Mindy said.

Mama Kay shrugged her shoulders, and then the two of them burst out giggling. The second woman and the man made their way slowly across the front yard. The woman carried her shoes in her hand. "I broke my heel," she said, holding her shoe out for Mama Kay to see.

"Eloise!" Mama Kay said. "I can't thank you enough for coming." They hugged with a little less enthusiasm, then Eloise took the man's arm and introduced him to Mama Kay. "Kay, this is my beau, Thomas Boyle. He drove us all the way from Atlanta."

"Thank you," Mama Kay said, shaking Thomas Boyle's hand. "It is a pleasure to meet you."

"The pleasure is mine." Mr. Boyle took off his hat and made a sweeping bow. He wore a light gray suit with a white shirt and a yellow tie, mirrored sunglasses. The hat was white felt and wide-brimmed. When he took it off Tyler could see that Mr. Boyle was bald as an egg, even though he did not look as old as Daddy Frank.

Mama Kay took the shoe from Eloise. "Tyler!" she said, "Run and fetch me some glue from your daddy's toolbox. Be quick, now, ya hear?"

Daddy Frank kept his tools in the garage and it was the one part of the house that was sacred to him and always kept in meticulous order. There was usually a car or two in the yard for Daddy Frank to work on when trucking got slow. Sometimes he'd buy a clunker and fix it up. Other times folks brought him theirs. The garage had but one window and it was gray with dust and cobwebs. It was cool and dark inside, and smelled of burnt oil and pipe tobacco. Tyler spent hours helping Daddy Frank, handing him tools and bottles of beer while Daddy Frank drank and cussed and worked. In the summer they tuned an old radio to the Braves games. In the winter, Tyler huddled up in front of a little electric heater. When Daddy Frank was on the road Tyler would sneak into the cabinets and read his collection of girlie magazines, Playboy, and Oui, and magazines without names at all, just numbers. Those were Tyler's favorites, and he would carry them down to the river where he and his friends looked at the girls and speculated about which ones they preferred and why, and what they would do with this one or that.

Daddy Frank kept his tools locked in a big Snap-On toolbox, but Tyler knew where the key was hid, and he found it and unlocked the box. Tyler found the glue, but before carrying it to Mama Kay he squeezed a little into a red mechanic's rag and held it to his nose. He breathed the fumes in deep and held his breath until his lips tingled and his tongue went numb. He felt dizzy and far away. He did this again and then, glancing towards the door, he climbed up on top of the toolbox and he reached in the cabinet where Daddy Frank hid his magazines. Standing on his tiptoes, he pulled two out of the stack and dropped them to the floor—one for now and one for later. He hid one in the bottom drawer of the toolbox and opened the other one. It was dark in the garage, but in the half-light Tyler could make out the figures of a man and woman on a bed. He thumbed through the pages until a Polaroid fell out of the magazine onto the floor. Tyler turned to the back of the magazine and found several more photos stuck between the pages. He looked closely at one. The picture was of a young girl naked on a blanket, evidently taken out in the woods someplace. Tyler looked around the room, then looked at the picture again. It wasn't anybody he knew. The man was middle-aged and white. The girl was young. He folded it back inside the magazine.

Tyler climbed back up the toolbox and threw the magazine behind the stack and closed the cabinet door. He lost his balance climbing down and fell, landing hard on his elbows and biting his tongue. He sat on the ground rocking back and forth, tasting blood and rubbing his elbows. Then he took the rag and inhaled another hit of glue. He remembered the picture that fell out of the magazine and he groped around the floor, but could not find it. He decided it must have slipped under the toolbox. The toolbox was on wheels but the bearings had rusted solid so even Daddy Frank couldn't budge it without help. Tyler stuck his arm underneath and felt around until he struck something cold and solid. Metal. He pulled it out—a pistol.

At first he thought he had found a hammer. Even when he got hold of it by the barrel he wasn't sure what he had. It wasn't sleek and pretty like the chrome-plated hell-blasters Daddy Frank lusted after at the pawn shop. This gun was L-shaped and clumsy-looking, rusted, and with what looked like a washer welded onto the butt end of the grip. The barrel was octagonal. Tyler took it in his hand and tried to raise it to arm's length, but it was so heavy he had a hard time holding it steady. He spun the chamber and, though stiff, it turned and set with a solid click. Tyler tried to cock it with his thumb but the hammer barely budged. He put his hand over it and leaned on it with all his weight and it slowly gave way. Tyler held it to the light and spun the chamber again. It was loaded.

By the time Tyler got back to the picnic Mama Kay had forgot all about him. He stood leaning unsteadily against the screen door from the kitchen, the glue loose in his left hand. His ears buzzed like a swarm of bees, his lips were numb and tingling, his eyes dilated. The light hurt.

"Will you fetch me a roll of paper towels, hun?" Mama Kay called. Tyler got one and trudged zombie-like to the picnic table and set it and the glue by her elbow.

"That your boy?" Mindy asked.

Mama Kay answered, "I guess he is now."

Tyler walked away and sat down cross-legged next to Jane and she smiled at him, covered her mouth and giggled. "What's the matter with you?" Tyler asked.

"Buggers," Jane said, pointing.

Tyler wiped a bit of glue off his nose. Jane knew what he had been doing because sometimes they did it together. "You better not tell," he hissed.

Jane had her slacks hitched up above her knees and scratched her legs with a chunk of Spanish moss.

"What are you doing that for?" Tyler asked.

"It's itchy," Jane said.

"Well, don't," Tyler said, yanking the moss out of Jane's hand and throwing it over his shoulder. "You'll catch chiggers."

"Chiggers?" Jane asked. She covered her mouth and giggled again.

"Come over here, boy, and let me take a look at you," Mindy called.

Tyler looked at her, but didn't move.

"Don't pay him no mind," Mama Kay said. "The boy likes to play the fool around adults."

Thomas Boyle frowned, then began to scold Mama Kay saying, "See here, Miss Kay, it's not right for a boy to disrespect his mother like that. I know his father wadn't much, but a boy needs a strong hand to keep him out of trouble. I suggest, if you aim to keep him, you let him know from day one that you are the law, and the law must be paid." He snapped his fingers and called, "Hey, boy! You hear your mama talking to you? Come over here like she says."

"Chiggers," Tyler said to Jane. "Remember when you got them itchy red bumps and Mama Kay had to paint you all over with fingernail polish to make it stop?"

"You deaf or somethin'?" Tomas Boyle said.

"Lookee what I found," Tyler said, and lifting the front of his shirt, he showed Jane the butt of the pistol.

Thomas Boyle stood up, and Tyler stood up, hesitated, then pulled out the pistol and swung it around in Thomas Boyle's direction. One of the churchwomen screamed and Mama Kay shouted, "Tyler, put that down!"

"That gun's not loaded," Thomas Boyle said, and he took a step towards Tyler.

There was a laundry line hung in the neighbor's backyard, behind and to the left of Thomas Boyle. Tyler took aim at a sheet and squeezed the trigger. The gun jumped in his hand and the sheet flew off the line, a big tear showing blue sky as the sheet crumpled to the ground. Jane clapped her hands over her ears began a long scream. The picnic guests scattered across the yard at a dead run. Some jumped the fence while others dashed around the corner of the house. Mama Kay and Thomas Boyle stayed put. Tyler cocked the pistol.

Thomas Boyle held out his hands in front of him and said in a sweet and low voice, "I know this is a hard time for you, boy. Maybe you should lay that gun down and we can talk about things man-to-man."

Mama Kay sipped her lemonade and sighed.

Tyler licked his lips and tasted blood and gunpowder. He took aim at a shirt and fired again. The shirt jumped and a hole appeared in the breast pocket. It dangled by one clothespin. Thomas Boyle ducked behind an oak tree shading the picnic table. He peeked around the tree and looked at Tyler.

Jane stopped screaming and stood up. She walked past Tyler and picked up another piece of moss, began rubbing her arms with it, then turned and went inside the house.

"Tyler," Mama Kay said softly, "please lay the gun down."

Tyler rubbed the barrel on his cheek. It was hot, but not enough to burn his face. He held the end of the barrel to his nose and inhaled. It smelled pungent, almost like glue. He cocked it again, looked into the cylinder and could see two more rounds. Thomas Boyle poked his head around the tree and Tyler took quick aim and fired.

He wasn't shooting to hit Thomas Boyle—the shot struck the tree well above him and showered him with bark and splinters—but Thomas took off running, anyway, screaming, "I'm shot! I'm shot!" Tyler was pretty sure he had missed, but he was glad to see Thomas Boyle jump into the Cadillac and peel away.

Mama Kay finished her lemonade and went inside the house.

Tyler laid the pistol down and went around to the garage. The guests were all gone, even Mindy and Eloise. Eloise had forgotten her shoes. Tyler opened the garage door and then closed it behind him, sat with his back to Daddy Frank's toolbox and began to cry. In a minute Mama Kay opened the door and asked him, "Hun, would you like some cake and ice cream?" He followed her into the kitchen.

The state trooper was the first cop to arrive. He pulled into the yard with his lights on but the siren off. Tyler could see through the window when he turned the corner on their block.

Mama Kay sat at the table fanning herself. She had stripped down to her slip and hung the black dress over the back of her chair. Tyler sat on one side of her, Jane on the other. The trooper knocked at the kitchen door. "Jane," Mama Kay said, "go to your room for a little while." Jane took her cake and ice cream, and with a long look over her shoulder, left.

The trooper came in without waiting for Mama Kay to answer. He was a big man, over six foot, and at least two hundred pounds. He looked young to Tyler, maybe twenty-five or thirty. He tucked his hat under his right arm. He wore his hair in a crew cut and it was shiny white, like Mama Kay's. He had smile lines around his eyes. Tyler saw that the holster on his hip was unsnapped. He carried Daddy Frank's pistol in his left hand.

Mama Kay had poured herself a bourbon and coke, and motioned to the trooper that he could have one too.

He shook his head. "Thank you, ma'am, but not while I'm on duty." He opened Daddy Frank's pistol and emptied the remaining shell from the cylinder. He held the gun up and read the markings. "We got us a Webley Mark IV, point four-five-five caliber. Don't see many of them anymore. Almost a antique. Used 'em in the First World War; British issue, or Canadian." Looking at Tyler he said, "Boy, what was you doing with this, anyhow?"

Tyler shrugged his shoulders. He could hear a siren, and in a moment another black and white came around the corner.

"He ain't right," Mama Kay said. "We buried his daddy today."

"I'm sorry to hear that."

The second cop pulled up into the yard and the siren cut out with a whine like a dying dog. In a minute a county sheriff came puffing up to the door, but the trooper waived him off. "Go home Sam, I got this under control."

The sheriff poked his head in the door and looked around. "Are you're sure?"

The trooper pulled out a chair and sat down across from Mama Kay. "I'll take care of it. You go on home." He and Mama Kay sat quietly, eyeing each other, until the sheriff was gone.

Tyler could see the neighbors beginning to congregate in their yards. Once in a while he could see somebody nod in the direction of their house. Then Mama Kay said, "He ain't gonna hurt nobody. He's just upset."

"That's likely the case, ma'am," the trooper said, "but dischargin' a firearm in the yard like that is a misdemeanor, and we gonna have to do somethin' about it."

Tyler had visions of swinging a scythe on the county road gang. He had cut weeds in the yard with Daddy Frank before and it blistered his hands. He wondered if Mama Kay would bring him cornbread and lemonade.

"But you ain't gonna put him in jail, are you? That ain't no place for a boy. He's not even twelve yet."

"The judge'll likely want to talk to the boy hisself. He ain't been in no trouble before, has he?"

Mama Kay shook her head. "Nothing any other boy in this county couldn't get caught for."

"Likely not then. But then again, he is his daddy's son. They might figure a little stay in the reformatory would do him good. They say a ounce of prevention is worth a pound a cure. But that's not up to me to decide. I suspect they'll want him to talk to a doctor or a psychologist or somethin'. But I got to take him in, for his own protection, if nothin' else."

Mama Kay squirmed in her seat. She set her elbows on the table, rested her chin in her hands, leaned closer to the trooper, and batted her eyes. "There must be something we can do?" she said. "Some kind of arrangement we can make? I would be very distressed if the boy went to jail the day we buried his daddy."

Tyler stirred the melting ice cream with his fork. He crumbled the pound cake into it and mashed it into a creamy paste. He looked at Mama Kay and saw the shadow of her cleavage practically shoved in the trooper's face.

The trooper leaned back in his chair and looked around. At length he asked, "Is there some place we could talk about this in private?"

Mama Kay stood up and took the trooper by the hand, led him down the hall to her room and closed the door.

When she was gone Tyler drank the rest of her bourbon and coke.

Jane came out of her room. "Is he gone?" she asked, and Tyler shook his head. Jane looked down and began scratching her arms. Tyler saw bright red welts running all the way from her elbows to her wrists. "I think I got chiggers," Jane said, and she lifted her dress and showed Tyler where welts started on her thighs.

It was getting dark. Most of the neighbors had given up gawking and gone inside. A mosquito fogger came down the street, its yellow light flashing. After it was gone, a sour smell lingered in the air. The telephone began to ring.

"You want to go for a ride?" Tyler asked.

"Where would we go?"

Tyler shrugged his shoulders. "I-o-know," he said. "Somewhere. Maybe Alabama."

Jane glanced towards Mama Kay's room. "Can you get the keys?"

"I don't need no keys," Tyler said. "Daddy Frank taught me how to start cars without 'em."

"Can you start a car without a key?" she asked.

Tyler nodded.

"Any car?" Jane asked.

Tyler's lips curled into a grin. "Any car at all."

Warriors

K'Sandra is crying in my office again. There is a small group of adults forming a circle around her. Some exhibit motherly, almost excessive concern, others bored indifference. Mrs. Moody, the school secretary, and Mrs. Casbah—the librarian (who never seems to find enough work to interfere with her gossiping) are among the former. The two motorcycle policemen, in helmets and boots, radios cackling, are among the latter. And there are a few students whose morbid curiosity led them to follow K'Sandra in from the outer office just so they could gawk.

K'Sandra is too big to cuddle, but Mrs. Moody wraps her arm around her the best she can in a gesture of motherly support. The motorcycle policemen shift their weight from one leg to the other, their handguns sticking out at odd angles. One of them plays with a set of stainless steel handcuffs. K'Sandra flinches. At her feet is a grocery bag. From where I sit I can see the shiny silver tops of cans, a clear plastic package of what appears to be macaroni, what must certainly be a sack of flour, and a fuzzy, hot-pink, stuffed toy rabbit.

I get up from my desk and motion towards the door. "Go on," I say, "get out!" waiving everyone out but K'Sandra, Mrs. Moody (who wouldn't have left anyway), and the policemen.

The policeman with the handcuffs reaches for K'Sandra's arm and grasps it firmly, but K'Sandra, all 240 pounds of her, tears away from him. She gathers the bag of groceries in her arms and tries to offer it to me. The bag, wet from the rain, disintegrates completely, and the contents tumble onto the floor. A can of lima beans rolls under my desk. Another rolls up to my left foot and stops. I look down at the pink fuzzy bunny.

When I took over as interim principal at Woodrow Wilson High it was only for a little while, and as interim principal, because though I held the doctorate degree, I lacked the ten years of administrative experience deemed requisite for the permanent position. I was only there to finish out the term. Be that as it may, I asked Mrs. Moody, the portly, middle-aged school secretary, to help me drag my desk around to the side of the office, where I could watch the rain, see the soggy winter leaves clinging to the tree outside my window. She thought it was strange and a waste of time, and when I tried to explain Feng Shui to her she was certain I was out of my mind. But it was my office—dammit—and I was going to do as I pleased, if only for a few months. After all, I was only the interim principal, and my replacement could put the desk on the roof for all I cared. That was five years ago and they still haven't found a replacement. Sometimes I think the big-wigs in the district office have higher priorities —other fires to stamp out, so to speak. Or perhaps they just can't fill the position.

This is why my predecessor left: Wilson has the lowest test scores of any high school in the state and the highest drop-out rate. It has the highest percentage of drug abuse, teenage pregnancy, and incidents of classroom violence. We have so many students (or former students) incarcerated, we call King County Jail a satellite campus. In short, Wilson High is a place administrative careers go to die. It has been the subject of two local television exposes and made *Time Magazine's* Worst Schools in America list. But "Woody," as the kids sing in their mock version of the school song, "stands tall." It does have a few redeeming virtues. It is a perennial basketball powerhouse, and the jazz band played at the governor's inauguration last year. That must count for something.

And there are the kids, many of them like K'Sandra. She is half-black, half-Samoan—big enough to play middle linebacker if the district would let her on the team. I believe she's tough enough, too, but instead she kneels, crying like a baby, on the floor of my office. This past fall she had the nerve to run for homecoming queen—and won. But her grades did not meet the minimum standards so I disqualified her, even though it set off a day of student protests. That meant that about twenty-five kids carried picket signs outside while about three hundred went home and got high (as opposed to getting high in the alley behind the gym). The rest stayed in class and probably had their most productive day of the year.

But it's not all bad. Mrs. Moody, who might have worked here since Wilson himself was president, is a joy to be around. She knows her job, does the lion's share of the work, and does it well. She coordinates the curriculum, files the transcripts, and handles parent's complaints. I might interview the new hires but nobody comes to work at Woody without Mrs. Moody's say-so. I'm basically a figurehead. And why not? Many of the parents went to Woody themselves, and they've known Mrs. Moody since they were kids. They know her better than they know me—and trust her. I'm white, middle-aged, and male. I'm the enemy. They wouldn't give me the time of day. And besides, I'm the interim principal. Why should they get to know me? I'll likely be gone in the next district shake-up. I doubt if Mrs. Moody would implement any changes I suggested anyway, changes outside of my office, that is. And I know better than to ask. She's bigger than me—and size is everything at Wilson.

Just ask K'Sandra. I once saw her knock a boy out with one punch for "disrespecting" her. I've read her juvenile files, even though they're supposed to be confidential. Once in a while the cops, parole officers, counselors, and etc. come around asking favors of me. They open their files and I open mine. Off the record, of course. We work around the system, and the truth is, it is helpful for me to know which kids are strung-out or in trouble with law. Yes, I have eyes and can pretty much figure things out on my own. But what my eyes can't tell me is who stole a car, delivered a controlled substance, fired shots into a teenage night club, assaulted a step-parent, or threw a bottle through the window of a department store. And that was just the stuff I know about from last summer.

But it's useful information—if for no other reason but self-preserva-tion. Take K'Sandra, for example. Her step-father's in the federal penitentiary in Walla Walla for sexually assaulting her. She has an anger problem—understandably so—and particularly towards men. She's been arrested twice for dealing cocaine and once for prostitution. So when she knocked out this kid, Jerome, for disrespecting her, Mrs. Moody and I had all these factors to take into consideration. Her anger is exacerbated by her issues, and by the fact that she is currently clean and trying to kick drugs. The temptation is to label her a bad seed and get rid of her. "A little leaven ferments the whole loaf," Mrs. Moody says.

We met with K'Sandra and we met with the boy, and we met with their parents together and separately. It's standard procedure. It was getting on towards seven o'clock when Mrs. Moody and I called K'Sandra and her mother into the office again. We hadn't had supper and we all were all tired and wanted to go home. We didn't want to expel her, but we couldn't say why. I was supposed to give K'Sandra one of those I'm-putting-my-job-on-the-line-for-you motivational speeches, but I couldn't bring myself to do it. Finally Mrs. Moody cleared her throat and asked K'Sandra, "Can you give me one good reason not to put your sorry butt out on the street where it belongs?" Tact was never her strong suit.

K'Sandra answered in a squeaky voice, "I'm tired Ms. M. Look at me. I'm fat, ugly, and I ain't goin' to graduate no how. Folks been tellin' me since I was knee high I wasn't goin' to 'mount to nothin'. I wake up every morning and I gots to fight just to get myself out of bed. But I decided a long time ago I was goin' to win that fight. I don't know why I hit that boy. I don't know why I do half the stuff I do. If somethin' gets in my way, I knock it down. If it gets up, I kick it. Tha's the only way I know how to live. But if I didn't, I would of died a long time ago."

Jerome's parents raised a stink, but K'Sandra stayed in school.

I think I do my job well. I keep a low profile with parents and haven't made community relations any worse than they were when I got here. I haven't ruffled the feathers of my superiors by asking for money or crusading for changes that wouldn't be popular with their suburban constituents. Best of all, I didn't start this mess, and as interim principal, nobody expects me to fix it. Still, I cannot help but believe that someday I will be the lamb whose sacrifice propels some righteous reformer into the superintendent's office.

I read a lot. I used to read academic journals for professional development. Lately I've been reading a lot of classic novels I never got around to in college; most recently, *Anna Karenina*. I attend a fair number of meetings downtown, and the occasional conference or seminar. Once in a while I'm called to testify about this or that—sometimes in court, other times before congressional committees investigating the mess we've got our educational system into. Nobody expects me to offer solutions, just excuses. With my thinning gray hair, wire-rimmed glasses, and rumpled suits, I'm a poster boy for the failures of our educational system. It appears I'm about to fail again.

The policeman gently places a hand on K'Sandra's shoulder but Mrs. Moody snatches it away. "You can't take my girlfriend," she says, and then turns to me. "You can't let him take him take her, Walter, you got to do something. You the principal here and you gots to stand up for your girls."

My girls?

K'Sandra's skin is chocolate brown, clear and pretty, her hair glossy black and kinky, she wears it pulled back in a neat bun. Her nose is wide and flat, her lips fat, her arms thick and strong as tree trunks, her eyes dark, glinting from the puffy folds of her face.

She has the most expressive face I have ever seen. I once caught her cutting up in the hall with her friends. She was dancing and improvising, imitating one personality after another—Oprah, Rosie, Brittany Spears. "You should go into the theater," I said. K'Sandra walked away without saying a word. I had forgotten the cardinal rule: they don't talk to us—especially not in the hallways, and never in front of their friends. I took this personally at the time, but after a while I got used to it. I suppose the kids learn young that if an adult talks to a child, it is only because the adult wants something.

But what I said was true. When K'Sandra is angry you can sense lightning crackling in the air. It makes you want to brace your knees for impact. And when she smiles it is like the summer sun breaking through after a hard winter of rain, and you expect to see a rainbow hovering somewhere over her shoulder. Now she's kneeling on the floor like a child sobbing over a dead puppy. I warned her that this would happen.

We have a maintenance man named Manuel who I do not believe speaks a word of English, though he seems to understand my instructions. One day I pointed out a leaking pipe in the gymnasium, and when I checked up on it I found he had plugged it with a wad of chewing gum. That's my job description. I am a wad of gum. Shortly after I took over the principal's office, Manuel installed one-inch thick, bulletproof glass panes in my windows. Then he installed bars over the windows, presumably to keep people from stealing the bulletproof glass. A lot of stealing goes on around here. Teachers carry one pen to school. Classrooms can't keep erasers for the chalkboards. We chain the toilet paper to the stalls. The kids still steal the toilet paper anyway. Sometimes they steal the chains.

Manuel was going to cut down the tree outside my window—it is an elm, I believe, or perhaps a sycamore. It is quite messy, always shedding bark or leaves or seedpods and such—but it is the only tree on the grounds. The only one. I was shocked when I realized this, and even more disturbed when I saw Manuel preparing to cut it down. I didn't order it cut. For all I know, Manuel wanted it for firewood for his house. But I'm sure he understood me when I jerked the chainsaw out of his hand and shouted, "NO!"

I'm glad we left it. I remember watching the leaves tumble in the fall, and the buds swell in the spring, a thin sheen of green appearing like a fine aura around the uppermost branches. And when school let out for the summer, I realized that I while I should have been busy making calls and sending out resumes, I had done nothing. I was in shock, a deer in the headlights. So I stayed on for another year.

K'Sandra looks up at me. Her nose is running, big tears well up in her eyes. "I was just doin' what you axed me," she says.

I have been called some names in the hallway, but conspirator and collaborator are not among them. "What do you mean, 'asked you'?" I say.

The policeman lets go of her shoulder and pulls his hand free of Mrs. Moody. He taps the handcuffs impatiently against his holster while his partner looks on.

Let me tell you about Wilson High. It has all the trappings of a real school. There is a flagpole out front and flags in most of the rooms, I think. We have desks, old ones, very small. The students sit on top of them more often than in them. The desks are colored, painted, or engraved with every imaginable form of gang graffiti and filth. We have an intercom with loudspeakers, and we make announcements every morning. We have a pep squad and a nurse, a jazz band, and a damn good basketball team. That's where the similarities end.

We have more security guards than any other school in the state, and still the hallways resemble a combat zone. It's bedlam. The staff huddles together in groups for protection. The students are on their own.

I have teachers who have forty-five kids in their classroom. How can you teach forty-five kids anything? I can't get substitutes, so if a teacher doesn't show up, the kids go to the library—if we're lucky. Sometimes they leave the campus and get high, wander around the neighborhood causing trouble. I wish I could say I blame them, but I can't. I can't conceive the mind-numbing tedium that makes up their day. The security officers try to keep them from getting out—but try to keep a kid from doing anything he or she really wants to do. You might just as well try to keep the wind from blowing through a screen door. Sometimes they come back for their next class, sometimes they don't.

There is an obeisance to politically correct multiculturalism. Once the Wilson Warriors—with a Native American Brave reminiscent of the old Indian Head Nickel for their mascot—we are now Warriors signified by a red capital W. Our hallway is adorned with multicultural Warriors of the World featuring Native Americans, African Tribesmen, Vikings, and a mural called "Warriors of Southeast Asia and the Pacific Islands." We even have an Eskimo warrior armed with a harpoon, though who he means to impale with it is not clear. I don't recall the Eskimo being a very warlike people. The kids mounted a campaign to change the mascot to

"The Woodies," as in Woody the Woodpecker, but their petition was dismissed by the district office, who surmised it might have a sexual overtone.

Did I mention we have metal detectors on our main entries to keep out guns? Of course, anyone who wanted a gun could just toss one in through one of the broken windows that go unrepaired all year. Contraband—weapons and drugs—finds its way into schools like this all the time. But after all, we are the Mighty Warriors.

"It was the earthquake in El Salvador," K'Sandra says. "You told me to buy some food for the relief effort—remember—only when I got to the store, I didn't have my purse, and I didn't have time to come back and make another trip 'cause I didn't want to be late for class. I knew it was wrong, but I knew they wouldn't trust no nigga to come back—so I was bringing you the things—like you said—and I was gonna give 'em to you and then get the money and take it back after school. Honest."

I look out the window and see a gang of kids across the street. I guess they are my kids, ditching class if they are. It's hard to tell sometimes. They are looking at my window and I imagine they are making disparaging remarks about me, the school, or authority in general. The kids don't talk to me very often. I can pretend that I am busy with administrative responsibilities and don't have time for them, but the truth is they don't talk to many adults, not any more than they have to, save a few special teachers who have been here a very long time. It is not cool to be seen talking with an adult. It is a cause for suspicion on the part of other kids, a sign of weakness. They make it clear, the delineation between us and them. They speak hip-hop. They practice effrontery. They elevate vulgarity to an art form.

I have a Monet reproduction on one wall of my office, "The Waterlillies," and I look away from K'Sandra towards the slightly-out-of-focus painting. It is, I think, the epitome of serenity, and when I get stressed-out I retreat to my office and look at it, think about my life, my future. I have a small CD player—not something that would invite theft—but enough to drown out the between-class hallway riots. I like classical music. If I listen real hard right now I can hear Ravel's *Tzigane*. I have a little water sculpture, too; a round ceramic bowl filled with smooth river stones with a statuette of an angel pouring water from an endlessly replenished chalice. The trickling sound is particularly soothing after a parent-student conference. Mrs. Moody snorted when I brought it in. "Some folks," she said.

"Look," says one of the officers, and I am struck by how deep his voice is. He is a tall black man, but skinny, and he doesn't appear to have the chest to resonate such a perfect baritone. "I know this unpleasant, but let's not make it any worse. I don't want to arrest the girl, but we have a problem with shoplifting in the area. The store owners blame the kids and, right or wrong, when the girl gets caught red-handed running out of QFC with a bag of groceries, I got no choice but to arrest her."

He sighs, bends down, and reaches for K'Sandra's hands again. K'Sandra tenses and flexes her arm. Her biceps are bigger than mine, and for the first time I notice that they are ringed with traditional Samoan tattoos.

Mrs. Moody grabs his hand again. "Listen here, Floyd..." she begins, and as soon as she grabs his wrist his partner comes at her. Just then K'Sandra reaches in her pants pocket with her free hand and we all jump, but she pulls out a wrinkled paper and offers it to the officer. He takes it with a wary look on his face. I look at his partner and see that he has unsnapped the strap fastening his pistol in his holster.

I used to sit in on classes but I gave it up because the students were unpleasantly demonstrative and the teachers seemed awkward and embarrassed. Now I let them do their jobs the best they can. I cover for them when they take a day off. I have just enough budget money to keep them sane, or at least, placated. The last straw never reaches the camel's back, the last shoe never drops, but disaster is never more than a rumor away.

I expected to be fired at the end of my second year, but perhaps there were wheels squeaking louder than Wilson's, and I was overlooked. I planned to quit at the end of my third year, but my foolproof escape fell through and I was left at the station while my train pulled away. At the beginning of my fourth year I renewed my commitment, but by mid-winter I was contemplating suicide. This morning I got a call from an old buddy of mine, Gordon Tannenbaum. Gordon has quietly worked his way up to superintendent of schools at an eastside suburban district.

He said: "Listen, Walter, I've got an opening for an assistant principal that came up unexpectedly. I can't go into all the details—confidentiality and all that—but I can fill it at my discretion—no candidates, no hearings, no board approval. Advance to Go, collect $200. Are you interested?"

"I'm interested."

"You'll be coming on board to help put out a fire, but it's not an out-of-control fire, and, hey, you're the best fireman I know."

"I don't know," I said, "sounds like I'm jumping out the frying pan..."

"Yeah, yeah, I didn't say it would be easy—but how much fun can it be working at a shit-hole like Wilson? I would think Wilson makes teaching citizenship at Sing-Sing look like a vacation."

"Maybe," I said, "Still..."

"I won't stick you for this, Walter, this is a favor-for-favor deal. Don't think of it as a lateral move, think of it as sidestepping. You take care of me, and I'll take care of you. We've got a new high school opening in two years, and if I can't get you the principal's job there, I can plug you in someplace else; scout's honor, Walter. You deserve better than Wilson—a man with your qualifications. The only catch is I need to know by Thursday at the latest. It even pays more," he assured me, and that's the sad truth. An assistant principal in the 'burbs makes more than a head honcho in the city. Interim head honcho, anyway.

Gordon's words stuck in my head—"a man with your qualifications." What qualifications? I've got a Ph.D. in Education and twenty hours of something called continuing education, which means I spent a few summers sitting in classrooms listening to professors harp on pedagogical theory, multi-cultural classrooms, reversing underachievement, and what-ever the current buzz-words were that year. I've got less than five years classroom teaching experience and, counting my five years at Woody, still less than ten in administration. I wonder, sometimes, if I know what I'm doing at all.

I've thought about doing other things. My wife passes this off as a mid-life crisis. "All men go through it," she says. "It's the little boy in you that still wants to be a pirate, or astronaut, or the center fielder for the Mariners."

K'Sandra looks at me, her chest heaving with suppressed sobs. "It's our assignment," she says. "About the earthquake. It says a thousand people died and they needed food and stuff. They was a mudslide, and they was lots of folks kilt, kids left with no parents or nothin'. That's why I got the bunny. I kept thinkin' about them little kids, and how scared they mus' be at night and all. I know you didn't say nothin' about no bunny, but I thought you would understand. I can pay you back if you be mad about

147

it."

I look at the Monet on my wall and remember a girl I knew in college who traveled to France the summer between our junior and senior years. She bought a bicycle and painted her way across Province. "Come with me," she said, and I was tempted. She was a willow-thin girl with long brown hair, given to wearing bandanas and long skirts. She liked walking barefoot, and making love in fields of wildflowers. I saw an article about her in the paper a while back—she had a show at a local gallery, and her work wasn't half-bad. The picture of her was hilarious—she wore an evening gown, her hair styled, a string of pearls around her neck, a few lines gracing the corners of her eyes. I suppose we all look different these days. In those days I was a wannabe guitar player with a garage band called The HumDingers that lasted almost a year. But instead of touring Europe I became a classroom aide with the Head Start Program—got a leg up on the volunteer hours I needed to get into grad school. It looked so good on my resume.

I suppose, in 1969, we all thought we could change the world. What I really wanted—deep down inside—was to sail. I wanted to own a little boat and take tourists out on fishing charters. Even better—and there was no such thing as ecotourism in those days—but even better was taking tourists whale-watching, or camping on deserted islands, or long, slow trips up the inside passage all the way to Alaska. Who woulda thunk it way back then, eh?

Did I mention that a State Department of Health and Social Services survey found that 75% of the girls at Wilson reported they had been sexually assaulted by the time they were eighteen? And 45% of the boys? "What does this mean?" I asked the researcher—an attractive young black woman just out of Columbia University. She shrugged. Her right ear was ringed with small silver hoops. "Perhaps they are being assaulted," she said. "Or they may think they are supposed to be, or that we want to hear that they were." Her hair was short. Her dress was African. The girls loved her.

Our school nurse is Mrs. Cantwell—her name a joke not lost on the students—but she is a competent nurse and clever and compassionate woman. I stopped by her office one morning and found her dispensing condoms. She was making sure, with graphic explanation, that the girls knew how to use them. This is strictly forbidden by district policy, which simultaneously abhors our high pregnancy rate and repudiates sex education. A fine policy for suburban girls, I am sure, who can afford to buy condoms at any drugstore and keep them hidden in their rooms, but not very effective for our girls, who often don't read English well, have no background in self-heath care, and have no privacy at home.

The girls disbursed from nurse Cantwell's office. As they brushed past me, one of them held up a condom in a silver foil package and kissed it. "We gonna have us some fun to-night!" she said, swinging her hips in an exaggerated swagger. Then she turned to me and rolled her eyes, tossed her hair. "Wha' chu lookin' at?" she said. The rest of the girls laughed, then hurried off down the hall.

The policeman is losing patience.

"Wait," I say, raising my hand. "She's right."

Mrs. Moody looks at me. The cop looks skeptical. "It completely slipped my mind," I say. "I meant to give her the money, but I just forgot. K'Sandra is a good kid and she means well…she just didn't want to be embarrassed in class, you know, by being the only one not able to help out. It's Mrs. Quintana's geography class, right?" I ask. I'm guessing, but K'Sandra nods her head vigorously. I see the cop looking at the homework assignment and I pray that I guessed right.

The cop looks at her with a doubtful expression on his face. "Where you work, girl?" he asks.

"Wal Mart" K'Sandra says, "in Renton."

"How you get to work? You got a car?"

I wince—I'm guessing if K'Sandra says, "Yes," he'll ask for her driver's license, or what kind of car she drives, and I'm pretty sure she doesn't have either.

But K'Sandra is nothing if not street-wise. She puffs out her chest and says, "I takes the bus."

"Which bus you take to Renton?" the cop asks.

"The one-six-nine."

"Look," I say. "How 'bout we walk back to the store and talk to the manager together. I'll pay for the groceries and see if I can smooth things over. I'm sure we can work this out. We'll send K'Sandra back to class—she won't go anywhere. And you know where to find her, if you have to. It's not like she's from out-of-town."

"And I know where you live, too, Floyd," Mrs. Moody says. "You think I don't remember you? I know what a mess-around you used to be. And that boy of yours, too."

149

Floyd holds up his hands in a gesture of conciliation. "I know," he says. "I was a kid once, too, but we all got a job to do. I tell you what. You keep your girlfriend out of QFC, at least until they forget about her, and I'll see what Mr. Walter and me can do to fix things up with the manager. But I ain't promising nothin', you hear?"

Mrs. Moody whisks K'Sandra away before Floyd can change his mind. I can't see where they went, but my money says it wasn't to class. I suspect Mrs. Moody will have a few words with her someplace private—the bathroom, maybe, or the teacher's lounge, and tonight she'll probably have a word with her mother. K'Sandra left the groceries on my floor, but she took the hot pink fuzzy bunny with her.

I turn my back on Floyd and stare out the window. There's a white Cadillac with tinted windows parked outside. I haven't seen this one before, and I make a note of it.

Floyd clears his throat. He drops K'Sandra's homework assignment on my desk and I see it was from Mr. Pierce's English class. I shrug.

"How long have you been here?" Floyd asks.

"Five years," I say.

He takes off his helmet and scratches his head. He's got a big bald spot on top.

His partner taps him on the shoulder and nods toward the door." Do you need me for anything?" he asks.

Floyd says, "See ya," and his partner leaves. Floyd sits down. "I graduated in '65," he says, and then, laughing, adds, "I was suspended three times my senior year. Mrs. Moody thought I would never get my diploma. I came back here after 'Nam and went through the police academy. The first time she saw me in uniform, I thought she was gonna die laughing. 'Look at you,' she said. 'The King o' Detention hisself.'"

I look outside and see the Cadillac is gone.

The radio cackles on Floyd's belt and he turns it off. He looks at his watch, then he looks at me. "Shall we go?" he asks.

I nod. Even though I should be calling Gordon and writing my letter of resignation, I get up and start for the door. I'll take care of all that tomorrow, maybe. If nothing else comes up.

Outside it has quit raining. Across the school parking lot I hear a whistle and the squeak of tennis shoes on the basketball court, a mixture of profanities and the guttural grunts of contact sport. I imagine that I will see K'Sandra in the hall tomorrow, and she will snarl at me and pretend that today never happened. She'll brag to her girlfriends that she stole from the store and talked her way out of trouble. But she might, just might, mind you, pay me back. And who knows? Maybe someday she'll right herself. Maybe I'll see her in in a grocery store, or somewhere around town. Or maybe she'll barge into my office someday and surprise me, wherever I am. Better yet, she'll bust into my office in a police uniform. Wouldn't that be a hoot? She come into my office in a uniform and stand there just like Floyd. I'd laugh until my sides split. I smile, picturing K'Sandra with a badge and a gun. She'd make a pretty good cop, too, I think.

The Couch

I was sitting at the table having dinner and catching up on my reading when my ex-wife called. Of course, I didn't know it was her until I answered. I laid the book on the table and the fork on my page and picked up the phone. "Hello," I said, and she said, "Hello, Sam."

I hate the way she talks to me. She has this West Texas drawl and her words seem to take forever being born. And when she talks to me I always feel like I've done something wrong—like I've been sent to the principal's office, again, and he's looking across his desk and sighing like I'm one of those kids who just never gets it—whatever *it* is.

Anyway, she said, "Hello, Sam," (like it's a real burden to talk to me) and I'm feeling guilty already even though I can't have done anything wrong. Our kids are grown. I don't owe her any money—my child support paid off years ago. I imagine she's standing in her kitchen and she's got the phone cord wrapped around her three times already because she's really high-strung (even if she talks slow) and gets worse whenever we talk. She's got long, thick black hair that tumbles down almost to the middle of her back, and black, black eyes, deep set in their sockets, with natural dark circles around them. She looks like she hasn't had a good night's sleep in her entire life, and I can picture her plucking at the phone cord like a one-stringed guitar and turning absent-minded circles until she's reached the end of her rope, so to speak.

I've got this paperback on the table entitled *Salt* by some guy from the Caribbean and it's half-assed interesting and I'd like to finish it. I've been trying to finish it for six months, but every time I pick it up it seems like something else comes along and gets in the way. And now she calls. When my ex starts something there's no ending it. So I said, "Hello, Linda, what's up?" because, after all, she wouldn't call me unless something was up, and she said, "Oh, nothing, really," which I know is a big, fat lie. "So how are you?" she asks, and between bites of mashed potatoes and gravy I said, "Fine."

"Listen," she said, "I brought a new living room set," And I answered

"Really?" not really giving a shit and wondering what I had to do with it and if she was just calling up to gloat. I felt like asking if she had run out of friends to talk to but I bit my tongue instead and said, "That's nice."

"So," she said, "I was wondering if you wanted to buy our old one."

"Buy our old one?"

"Sure," she said. "I'm asking $500 for it. That's a really good deal and I thought I would offer it to you first."

It's not a really good deal and I'm sure I'm the last person she knows that she hasn't offered it to. But I remember the couch real well. It has a nice cream-colored background stitched through with soft lines of colored pile—light blue, rust, brown, orange. The overall effect was to give it a deep beige color, from a distance, but it was pleasing to look at, especially up close. It had nice low arms of a dark walnut, I believe, and it looked good, that cream-color with the dark wood arms. We bought the couch from a store in Walla Walla that was going out of business and only had one piece left of a two-piece set. We looked all over for the love seat that went with it and eventually found a match in Hermiston, Oregon, so we bought it and strapped the box on top of our Mercury Zephyr and drove some hundred-odd miles home at about 45 miles an hour. It was hot, and I remember stretching our legs and drinking cold apple cider at a roadside stand where a bunch of little Mexican kids played soccer in a flat, bare field strewn with dirt clods. The cottonwoods were in bloom and even though it was 99 degrees outside and the sun flamed in a brilliant blue sky, it looked like a blizzard where we were standing, a summer-time blizzard of cottonwood fluff. We picked cottonwood fluff out of that loveseat for years.

And I remember that we found tiny worm-holes bored into the walnut arms. They didn't seem to hurt anything, and they had been there for a while—they were varnished over—but it seemed odd, and we worried that the worms were alive and would eat up all our furniture. We didn't have a lot of money in those days, and a little thing like buying living room furniture was a big deal to us. I welded trailer hitches and she waited tables and it takes a lot of pancakes and trailer hitches to pay for a couch. When we found the holes I remember us sitting there, hip to hip, staring, thinking, tracing them with our fingers.

When we brought it home we made love, "breaking it in" we called it, and we fell asleep that way. And when we woke up the soft thread piles had made pink indentations in our skin. We were spotted like leopards, and Linda got the idea that we could play connect-the-dots with lipstick and so we painted ourselves all over in a burgundy mosaic and chased each other around the house. In the morning I couldn't get all the lipstick off and when I went to work everybody wondered what the heck was wrong with me—was I coming down with something? I told them I was allergic to tofu and ate some by mistake in Chinese take-out.

I remember Linda the summer she was pregnant and it was hot as hell and we didn't have any air conditioning. She laid on the couch and she was so sick—just miserable—and I used to fan her on the weekends and make fresh lemonade—she craved lemonade—and we would listen to "A Prairie Home Companion" on the radio. "It's been a quiet week in Lake Wobegon ..."

And I remember the day I came home from work and found writing on the arm. My daughter had written all over it with a ballpoint pen. Of course, the ink didn't show, but the pen engraved every word in the woodwork. I called her into the living room and she denied it—blamed it on her little brother—but he was only a year or so at the time, and we both knew he didn't do it. It was a nice try, but I spanked her anyway. She's twenty-two, now, and has a son of her own.

I pushed a piece of pot roast around the plate with my fork and lost the page in my paperback.

"So, what do you think?" Linda asked, and I chewed a little while and thought it over.

It was a pretty good old couch, all right, and my wife, my ex-wife, I knew took good care of it. She was a fanatical housekeeper. Whenever she would get mad she would clean the house. She dusted everything, even the light bulbs. She washed the shelves in the closets. Then she would vacuum —"Hoovering," she called it—a word I didn't hear again until I visited Ireland. We had a spotless house. Even the couch.

Well, almost spotless. If you look real close I could show you where my son spit out his cough medicine when he had the flu. And if I remember right there's a coffee stain on the middle cushion from when I jumped up and ran out of the house the time he wrecked his bike down the street. He did a face-plant on the asphalt and took half the hide off the right side of his head, poor little guy. He did it again a month later, but he never gave up. He rides dirt bikes today, and he's fearless.

And I remember walking home one evening, when the car ran out of gas down the street, and finding the door unlocked and the house dark.

There was an old jeep parked in the driveway and when I came in I could hear the tinny sound of a cheap transistor radio playing in the living room. Don McLean was singing "Bye, Bye, Miss American Pie," and my daughter was on the couch making out with her boyfriend, and the house was dark and they didn't know I was standing in the kitchen watching. I wanted to kill the little son-of-a-bitch, but then I remembered that I was young and in love once, too, so instead I snuck back outside and took a long walk. When I finally came home I made a lot of noise in the entry, stomping around knocking imaginary mud off my boots, and when I walked in they were sitting hand-in-hand and looking decent, if a little flushed in the cheek.

I couldn't tell you how many hours I spent on that couch doing math homework with my son. He didn't like school. He never seemed to fit in or catch on. I had to work a lot those days, and I depended on Linda to keep him lined-out, but she was a high school dropout herself and didn't take much interest in the kid's schooling. I remember once he made a "D" and the teacher sent home a note that he was close to failing. I told him I'd give him fifty dollars if he raised his grade to a B.

"What will you give me if I make an A?" he asked.

He might just as well have asked me what I'd give him to paint the moon pink, but I told him I'd give him a hundred dollars. Even though I missed a car payment, it was the best hundred dollars I ever spent.

Towards the end I got to know that couch pretty good. I spent a lot of nights on it, wrapped up in a blanket, listening to the clock tick. I had time to relish every stain and scratch. It was soft, that couch. It had these nice end pillows that were cylindrical—rolled up like a cotton burrito. When I slept on them my neck felt good. After a while those pillows like to wore out.

I left that house one spring day with two suitcases and a radio, and it was all I ever got. I didn't get a blanket or a pillow, not my tools, my winter clothes, not even my camera (which Linda didn't know how to use). I left her a nice house in the country all but paid for. I could have sued for half, but I let it go. I told myself it was for the kids, and in a way it was, but when it came to Linda I might just as well have argued with the wind.

"You know," I said at last, "when I moved out I gave you that couch."

"You didn't give it to me," Linda said, her voice rising half-a-hundred decibels. "It was mine."

I got an old couch in my living room that's ugly as a bruise and has a low spot in the middle big as death valley. The hide-a-bed part broke and hangs down onto the floor. If I sleep on it the springs burrow into my back and I wake up feeling like I been used for a hockey puck. My apartment's hot in summer and cold in winter. I've got crack heads for neighbors downstairs. If I leave my dishes in the sink when I go to work they're covered with roaches when I come home. I look out my window in either direction and I see concrete and sky for as far as the eye can see, one as gray as the other.

"You keep it," I said at last, "or sell it. Get rid of it. Throw it out. Give it to charity. I don't care, but thanks for asking." She said, "Okay," and I hung up and sat down. After a minute, I picked up the book. I thumbed through the pages, looking for the place where I left off reading. After all, it's only a couch, right?

The Number You Have Reached

You walk into a diner at nine o'clock Sunday morning smoking a fat Torpedo Figurado and carrying a $350 bottle of Sol Añejo tequila. The diner is empty. There is a long, white counter stretched out to your right. A half-dozen, crappy, orange-upholstered booths line the wall to your left, with as many tables in between, but not a customer in the place. The floor is grimy. Most of the tables are piled with dirty dishes. You pick the cleanest spot you can find on the counter, right next to the cash register, and sit down on one of those roundy-round stools with the chrome-plated footrests. You prop your elbows on the Formica. It is cool and slightly greasy. You take a swig from the bottle and almost finish it. It's your second bottle since you swiped a Conde Nast fake-leather backpack from an open Corvette convertible last night. You didn't know there was tequila and cigars in the backpack, you just got lucky. You kept the goodies but ditched the backpack right away. The booze doesn't even burn your gut anymore. You set the bottle down on the counter with a satisfying twack. There is a radio playing faintly from the back room. You pick out the strains of Kenny Rodgers and Dolly Parton crooning "Islands in the Stream."

The grill is on. There are two pots half-filled with black, rendered-down coffee on electric burners directly in front of you. There are cooked link sausages piled on a towel by the grill and crisp, dry bacon stacked on a plate beside them. You smell the meat and your mouth waters. You haven't eaten in more than a day. "Hello?" you say. You take a puff off the cigar and exhale in the direction of the grill. Kenny and Dolly ask, "How can we be wrong?" Offhand, you can think of about five hundred ways. You get up and walk around the counter and peer into the back room.

The cook is sitting on a five gallon plastic bucket with his feet up on another bucket and his back against the wall by the walk-in cooler. The door to the cooler is open. He is smoking a cigarette. He has a Lone Star long-neck clenched between his knees, and a half-dozen empties scattered at his feet. The air above him is hazy. There is a mountain of butts on the floor. Under his apron he wears a sweat-stained tee shirt and some grubby jeans.

You drum your fingers on the door and clear your throat. "Good morning," you say.

"Fuck you," he replies.

"Rough day?" you ask.

"Let me tell you about a rough day," he says, rising. You wish you hadn't asked.

He chugs his beer and brushes past you into the front room. He takes a swig of your tequila—empties it—then flings the bottle through the plate glass window just above and slightly to the right of the faded red letters that say Julia's Home Cooking. The letters had green and gold outlines, and some holly and berries trim left over from Christmas. Or maybe it was lettuce and tomatoes. The paint was faded and the artwork iffy. The bottle punches through the window and the glass cascades onto the sidewalk outside and startles a cat that was stalking a pigeon. The cat goes one way and the pigeon the other. You think they have the right idea.

The cook turns and makes like he's going to stab his finger into the middle of your forehead.

You ask, "Can I have a cup of coffee and a menu?"

The cook stops, his arm coiled snakelike in mid-strike. He unties his apron and tosses it on the grill, walks into the cooler and comes out lugging a case of Lone Star on his shoulder. "Fuck you," he says again as he passes, "and your coffee." As an afterthought he pauses and scoops a handful of bills from the till and stuffs them in his jeans pocket. After he leaves, the apron begins to smoke.

It is July and already 95 degrees outside. The clock on the wall says nine oh five. There is no traffic on the street. The tequila is fading and you feel a world-class hangover coming on. Six months ago you left your wife and daughter in Burlington, Vermont. You'd been drinking for forty-eight hours and your wife had been complaining about it for forty-seven. You told her you were going to the store for a bottle of milk and a newspaper. Instead you bought another bottle of Cuervo and drove to New Jersey, where you stopped under a freeway and sold the tires off your car for $100. You bought another bottle from Tiki's Liquors because it was close and a Greyhound ticket to Atlanta because your car wasn't going anywhere without tires.

"Hello," you say, but there is no sound except the drone of the compressor in the AC. That, and the music from the back room.

You come around the counter to the grill and pick up the apron, which is smoking but not yet burst into flames. You wipe down the grill with it and throw it away. Dolly and Kenny stop singing. You are listening to 88.6 Country Proud. Soybeans are down a nickel. The National Weather Service is forecasting another drought. Corn weevils have reached epidemic proportions.

You pour yourself a cup of coffee and it is bitter as bile, so you pour half of it out and fill it back up with milk and sugar. It's still bad, but you drink it anyway. When you get to the bottom of the cup the sugar washes the burnt taste away. You open the little fridge under the counter and find a pitcher of OJ next to a carton of eggs and a white plastic tub full of grated potatoes.

There is a mountain of hash browns on the grill and a half-dozen eggs sizzling sunny side up when the first customer walks through the door. He sits down where you were sitting and looks around. Just for kicks you plop a menu in front of him, give the counter a half-hearted swipe with a wet rag, and pour him a glass of water. "What'll you have?" you ask.

"Waffles," he says.

"Can't," you reply. "Iron's broke."

"Pancakes then."

You don't remember seeing batter in the cooler but you look anyway. "Out of batter," you say.

"What have you got?"

"Eggs."

You serve him eggs and hash browns, throw in a side order of sausage for free. You pour him a cup of coffee but he complains about it. You take his cup, taste it, then pour half of it out and fill it back up with leftover milk from a glass on the counter. Then, while he watches, you fill the cup with sugar until it overflows.

"That's disgusting," he says.

On his way out the door you say, "Ya'll come back now, ya here?" You go to the cooler and open a beer. You eat the eggs and sausage.

After a while a very old woman in a blue granny dress and black, square-toed shoes hobbles in. She is wearing a plastic, imitation straw hat covered with small, pink plastic flowers. She walks with a stainless steel cane. She shuffles to the booth in the furthest corner and sits down, raps the table with her cane, says, "Julius, I'm home." She stares into space. You ignore her.

A minute later two men come in. One is tall and thin, dressed in a black suit with a white shirt and string cowboy tie. He wears a ridiculously small black cowboy hat with a silver Navajo band around it. He reminds you of a mortician you knew when you were a child.

The other man is in a wheelchair. He wears a genuine Panama hat and a green Hawaiian shirt with blue parrots printed on it. He has a plaid blanket over his knees. He wears dark glasses. He is older, sixty maybe. His face is bony, skeletal.

A kid comes to the door on a skate board, leans in, says, "Nasty," then boards away. His hair is orange. You hate the sound of skates on pavement.

You finish your beer and look around for your cigar. You find it. It is still lit and you take a deep, satisfying puff and exhale a cloud of blue smoke. The old woman raps the table with her cane. The men look around at the mess. After a while you pick up an order pad and saunter over to their table. "Hiya, creeky," you say to the man in the wheelchair. "What'll ya have?"

"This table's dirty," he says.

"No shit?" you reply.

You go behind the counter and find a gray plastic bus tub. You pick it up and get a wad of old, warm butter on your hand. You put it down and wipe the butter on a rag. You can still feel it under your nails. You return to the table and pile the dishes, glasses, cups, and silverware in the tub and wipe the table down. You empty the tub into the garbage. The glasses break. The old lady raps her cane on the table. The kid skates by on his board again. You notice that his orange hair is worked up into shiny spikes. He is wearing a bright, steel chain around his hips. You presume he wants to look tough. You wonder how long it takes him to make up his hair. The men order bacon and eggs.

Somewhere in Appalachia you left the Greyhound to spend the weekend in a cabin by a lake with an albino girl named Carol. Carol got on the bus while you were sleeping. In Virginia, maybe. She promised that it was beautiful and said it once belonged to her father, but he had sold it to a US Senator from Idaho who lived in DC and used it for a love nest. She said he used to bring his interns there to make home porno movies. She didn't tell you how she knew this. She had pink eyes. Even her pubic hair was white.

The cabin had one room, no electricity, no furniture. There was nothing to eat except some beef jerky you found, evidently forgotten at the back of the top shelf of the cabinet. You fucked dog-style on the floor. You got splinters in your knees. The roof was covered with dead leaves and green mold. The outside boards weathered gray. It leaned to the south.

The lake was pond-sized and scummy. Cattails overran the shallows and lily pads smothered everything else. You paddled around naked in the afternoon in a tipsy rowboat. It was her idea. You tried to make love but the mosquitoes ate you alive. The boat seeped amber water. It smelled froggy. When you ran out of tequila you walked to town to buy more. You stopped in the bar for a cool one. You forgot your way back. After a while you gave up looking and bought a bus ticket to Knoxville. You were disappointed not to have found any movies of the senator.

Willie Nelson is singing "Blue Eyes Cryin' in the Rain" on the radio. You scramble the eggs with the shells and burn the toast. You serve it to the two men, but they don't seem to notice. "We need to talk," they say. They gesture towards an empty chair.

"Would you like a beer?" you ask.

They nod.

While you're in the cooler you think about the possibilities.

"Things aren't working out," says the man who looks like an undertaker.

"I guess not," you reply.

"We're going to have to take a new direction."

"I'm not very good at directions," you say.

They look at each other.

"Do you understand what we're saying?" they ask, together.

First you nod. Then you shake your head.

You were sleeping in the doorway of a pawnshop near the civic center in downtown Knoxville at two o'clock in the morning when a policeman tapped you on the foot with his nightstick and asked what you were doing.

You told him you wanted to be first in line to buy Elvis memorabilia in the morning.

He told you to move along.

You stretched and told him to fuck himself.

He and his partner threw you in the river. Then they arrested you

Melvin Sterne

for swimming after dark. It is illegal to swim in the Tennessee River within the city limits of Knoxville after dark. The fine was $50. Someone called your wife and she paid it. Evidently there was a "Missing Person Report" on you. The cops ask what's what and you tell them you're not missing a thing. Your wife cried on the phone. She said your daughter missed you. She wanted you to go to treatment. She said her father would foot the bill. You know he hates you. You think he might bribe the nurses to put meds in your food and keep you forever. You think about Jack Nicholson in *One Flew Over the Cuckoo's Nest*. The cops take you to the Salvation Army Mission while your wife goes to wire you a plane ticket home.

That afternoon you hit the jackpot panhandling and bought a bottle of La Pinata. You hitched a ride to Tulsa with a meth-addicted trucker named Phil. He stopped in Little Rock and wanted you to suck his dick. He pulled his pants down around his ankles and tried to get hard and put on a condom. You ran away with his wallet. He looked funny chasing you down the highway and pulling up his pants at the same time. You think it served him right.

"Perhaps we're not being clear," says the man in the wheelchair. "Let me try a different approach. May I call you Larry?"

You shrug your shoulders. "Sure."

The men look puzzled.

"Your name is Larry, isn't it?" asks the undertaker.

"That depends on who's asking," you say. "Are you with the IRS?"

They shake their heads.

"Then I might be Larry. I could be Larry."

The man in the wheelchair pulls a pistol from under the blanket and you lunge for it. The two of you tumble onto the floor. You have almost pried the gun out of his hand when the undertaker crashes a chair across your back. Unlike in the movies, the chair does not break. Your back does not break, either, but it hurts like hell. You flip the pistol away from the wheelchair man with what you think might be your last, dying breath. The undertaker kicks you and you feel something snap in your hip. He straddles your back and pounds your head with his fists. You force your-self onto your hands and knees and find a steak knife on the floor miraculously close to your left hand. You jab the undertaker in the meaty part of his right thigh. He rises like a shot. You expect something bad to happen but nothing does. The undertaker hops out the door howling.

164

Creeky rights his wheelchair and hefts into it. One wheel wobbles wildly as he leaves. The old woman beats the table furiously with her cane. In sports, the Mets beat the Cardinals nine to three. Carlos Beltran hit two home runs including a grand slam in the pivotal fifth.

You stagger to the door. Your hip hurts too bad to run. Outside, the boy with the orange hair sprawls on the sidewalk. His skateboard is upside down. The wheels are spinning. Creeky's wheelchair lies on its side. One wheel has fallen off. There is a trail of blood spots leading to an empty parking space. A black Lincoln trailing blue smoke peels around the corner.

You look at the orange headed kid.

He sits up. "Gnarly," he says. He is wearing a dog collar. His face is scratched.

You remember that you are on your way to Seattle. You think it might be a good time to leave but you can't resist the temptation to snag a six-pack of beer. It might come in handy—especially since Larry (you presume he was Larry) finished off your tequila. On your way to the cooler you check the till to see if Larry missed anything. He took all the bills, but you scoop a cool handful of quarters. You hit the cooler and snag a six pack of Lone Star. When you come out of the back a policeman blocks the front door.

When you left Little Rock, you hitch-hiked north until you hit Saint Paul. You thought a change of scene might do you good. In Saint Paul you worked two days at a farmers' market. They paid you in cash and vegetables. On the second day you emptied the till and hopped a west-bound freight. You took three bottles of Patron and a bag of limes with you, but you forgot the salt. Still, it was better than nothing. The next night, in Cheyenne, a hobo climbed into your boxcar. He told you his name was Willie and he was a famous bluesman. He said he had a hundred-dollar harmonica but he wouldn't show it to you. He did show you pictures of his family. They were all ugly as sin but you didn't tell him this. "They understand me," he said. His wife had a boyfriend, but he slept on the couch in the winter when Willie came home. You said that was considerate. That's the exact word you used. Considerate. After you and Willie killed the last bottle, you took turns throwing limes at cows grazing near the tracks.

You told Willie about your daughter, Angelina, and how she loves you unconditionally. She brings you beers from the fridge. You taught her the labels so she could tell one brand from another. You tell her, "Bring me a Tecate," and she brings you a Tecate. Your wife does not approve of this. Willie nods sympathetically. "Women," he says. While you are sleeping off the tequila, he steals your jacket and what's left of your money. You wake up lonely in Bonners Ferry. That's where you find the Corvette with the Conde Nast fake-leather backpack with the bottles of Sol Añejo and the Figurados. You wished it had more than two bottles, but beggars can't be choosy. Still, you call the owner a "fucking cheap bastard."

The policeman asks you for some ID and you tell him about Willie and the train ride from St. Paul and how you lost your wallet. He is not impressed. Not even with the bit about the harmonica. They fingerprint you at the lock-up. You tell them your name is Jefferson Davis and you are a US Senator from Idaho. They bring in the old woman but she doesn't know where she is, much less who you are. They ask if you've ever been arrested before and you think about telling them about swimming after dark in the Tennessee River. You decide not to tell them. The cops are perplexed. Evidently there is no longer a "Missing Person Report" out on you. They check their computer and smoke some cigarettes without offering you one.

Since you didn't take anything tangible, they can't bust you for stealing. You tell them you panhandled the quarters but nobody cares about them anyway. The café owner doesn't know you from Adam. He says he hired a fry cook named Larry to run the breakfast shift. You claim you were beat up by a man in a wheelchair. Nobody believes you, even though they have the wheelchair. They show you the pistol and ask if you know anything about it. You tell them it is safer standing behind it than in front of it. They charge you with destruction of property. They take your shoelaces and your belt.

You tell them you know your rights and you are entitled to make a phone call. You swagger when you say this. You've watched enough TV to be confident in matters pertaining to the law. They take you to a pay phone in the hall. You think it is about time to check in with your wife and tell her you are all right. You call collect. You get a recording. "The number you have reached is no longer in service..."

"That's odd," you say.

You call your father-in-law, in Camden, but he won't take a collect call. You know he is a cheapskate so you call him again on your dime. It actually costs two dollars for the first three minutes. "Robert," you say.

"It's me, Sid. You're not going to believe this, but I can't get through to Susan." Robert hangs up and the phone eats your quarters. The guard looks at you. "I see," you say. "That bad? A whole week, huh?" You cover the mouthpiece and say to the guard, "Big storm back east, phone lines are down."

Across the hall is a door with a little window of wire-reinforced glass in the middle of it. Inside you see the orange-headed kid talking to a couple of cops. They've emptied the kid's pockets and you see an i-pod, some change, and what looks like a tube of glue.

"Well," you say, "I'll try again later. Tell her I'm in jail in Bonner's Ferry and I need her to post bail."

When you hang up the cop says you're in Pocatello, not Bonner's Ferry. You shrug it off. One place is as good as another. He asks if you want to call anybody else. You can't think of anybody in particular. You got fifty cents in your pocket. A local call is seventy-five.

www.ingramcontent.com/pod-product-compliance
Lightning Source LLC
Chambersburg PA
CBHW031320280626
47169CB00019B/2334